Praise for Rebecca Harrington's

Soci*a*ble

"Illuminated against a hilarious and satirical backdrop, Harrington writes about navigating digital media in the workplace, handling a bad breakup (through equally worse online dating), and what feminist friendships look like after college."
—*Nylon*

"In *Sociable*, we get a taste of [Harrington's] signature wit courtesy of main character Elinor Tomlinson, who shows up to New York City with journalistic aspirations, but has to work for a lousy old website (gasp!)."
—Clever

"A young woman traverses her twenties and the toxic land-scape of New York media in Harrington's novel of millennial manners. . . . Harrington captures the oppressive narcissism and frustrated ambitions of Elinor's world with nauseating accuracy. Frothy on the surface with teeth underneath."
—*Kirkus Reviews*

"Harrington casts her story in the mold of the old-school novels of Thackeray and Fielding. . . . [She's] got media-based youth culture down cold."
—Shelf Awareness

"Hilarious and bold, *Sociable* is a perfect send-up of our social media–obsessed culture."
—Emily Culliton, author of
The Misfortune of Marion Palm

Rebecca Harrington

Soc*i*able

Rebecca Harrington is the author of the novel *Penelope* and the comic essay collection *I'll Have What She's Having*. Her work has appeared in *New York* magazine, *The New York Times*, *Elle*, NPR.com, and other publications. She lives in New York City.

Sociable

Sociable

A NOVEL

Rebecca Harrington

VINTAGE CONTEMPORARIES

VINTAGE BOOKS

A Division of Penguin Random House LLC

New York

FIRST VINTAGE CONTEMPORARIES EDITION, FEBRUARY 2019

The Library of Congress has cataloged the Doubleday edition as follows:
Name: Harrington, Rebecca, author.
Title: Sociable : a novel / Rebecca Harrington.
Description: First edition. | New York : Doubleday, 2018.
Identifiers: LCCN 2017025266
Subjects: LCSH: Dating (Social customs)—Fiction. | Social media—Fiction. |
Internet—Fiction. | GSAFD: Humorous fiction.
Classification: LCC PS3608.A78196 S67 2018 | DDC 813/.6—dc23
LC record available at https://lccn.loc.gov/2017025266

**Vintage Contemporaries Trade Paperback ISBN: 978-0-8041-7217-2
eBook ISBN: 978-0-8041-7219-6**

www.vintagebooks.com

Printed in the United States of America
10 9 8 7 6 5 4 3 2 1

To my mother—my greatest ally, my moral compass, and my favorite conversationalist. I couldn't have done anything without you.

Between what matters and what seems to matter,
how should the world we know judge wisely?

—E. C. BENTLEY

Sociable

Chapter 1

Facebook: An article called "15 Images of a Sloth That Will Just Make You Laugh." Comment: "Mike Moriarty [hyperlinked] I feel like you are totally number 7." Elinor posted this at 4:00 p.m. on a Tuesday. It was liked thirty times, mostly by relatives.

Twitter: 30 tweets. A sample: "This is why Marianne Goodacre is my favorite writer." The link is to a quote about writing being difficult but also rewarding. It was favorited two times by people Elinor didn't really know that well.

Instagram: 2 pictures. Picture 1: An attenuated, wolfish-looking animal, a dog. The dog is collapsed on the sidewalk and tied up to a fire hydrant with a yellow nylon leash. Its legs are somewhat contorted on the ground. There is a sepia-tinged filter on the picture that gives it an oddly flat quality. For example, an irregular blob of gum is somehow in hyperfocus—the same as the dog. Caption: "Mike saw this lil guy just chilling out near our Sunday brunch spot. #goals." It was liked fifteen times.

Picture 2: Elinor and her boyfriend (Mike). It's a selfie. They are smiling on what seems to be the Brooklyn Bridge (there are brownstones, industrial water, and cables behind them). Elinor has her arm slung around Mike's neck. She is kissing his cheek. It is a very flattering picture, of Elinor especially. Her jaw looks thin. Caption: "Walking across the Brooklyn Bridge for our anniversary #lovethisguy #brooklynlyfe #bkbridge." It was liked twenty times.

. . .

t was midway through the party and everyone was drunk in a professional but sloshing way, when we saw Elinor, hovering near a table, holding her coat. The table had three red bowls on it, filled with identical anemic chips. Elinor took a chip out of one of the bowls and ate it. No one had done something like that during the entire preceding hour.

We were in a small backyard dotted with the occasional tuft of stodgy, bulbous grass. A Twister tarp lay discarded under a tree, getting dirtier as people stepped on it. Lights with large filaments dotted the railings, which gave the gathering an aesthetic that recalled other parties in the same general milieu, and existing pictures.

The party was celebrating or mourning the fact that the Newr Report, a news website (www.newrreport.com/news), was going out of business. It was going out of business because it hadn't ever made money. Websites couldn't go on forever in that kind of environment—but it did go on for a fair bit of time. And when you took it all together, there were twelve years of events collected in some ineffable space somewhere. So it wasn't nothing.

Elinor twisted a bit of her hair in two fingers. She had been alone near this chip table for a long time and she knew no one at the party. Her coat was so heavy and made out of felt. Mike was gone. Was he in the bathroom, inside the house? He had said he wanted to get a drink. She had already looked at Instagram. She had already read an article on her phone. She had already texted two people. She had already been in the proximity of others and not talked to them (it was why she was at the chip table in the first place). How much more could she do?

A vulpine cat sauntered between Elinor's legs. It had been wandering the party the entire evening. It was Andrew Newr's cat, and as such, it had a kind of notoriety. The cat had an Instagram account, for example, in which it would sometimes travel to Malta or lie curled on a bed. Elinor bent close to the cat and trained her phone on it. The cat immediately sprinted away, to hide under another metal-legged chip table about ten feet away.

"I've been trying to take a picture of that cat all night," said a girl who had been standing near Elinor this entire time but not talking to her. She had been talking to a guy wearing a crumpled blue shirt and crumpled brown pants. "That cat is so cute. That cat was everywhere at that office. I can't fucking believe it."

"I was going to caption the picture #partycat," said Elinor, shyly.

"OMG, that's funny," said the girl. Elinor dropped her coat on the ground, next to the chip table, kicked it under the table, and got dirt on it.

"So, did you guys work at Newr Report?" said Elinor.

"No," said the girl. "But I knew people that did. It's so so so sad."

"I know," said the guy. "It's really extremely fucked up. Late capitalism."

"The cat is back." Elinor could see the cat slinking out from underneath the other chip table. Other people, people next to that chip table, started taking pictures of the cat and the cat bowed to their lenses, and seemed to smile at them bashfully.

"That cat is like, basically a meme," said the girl. "A meme that hated you."

The guy laughed at that, crumpling his shirt more.

"Memes are always of like, a grumpy-faced thing. I don't think the cat hated me," said Elinor.

"Attention," said the founder of the Newr Report, Andrew Newr. He had emerged on a deck that jutted in a Scandinavian fashion from the back of his house. He was extraordinarily thin. Odd bones emerged from his face that Elinor had never seen before on another human person. One under his eye— another in his forehead. Where was Mike?

"Thank you all so much for coming." Andrew Newr cleared his throat. "I wish I was surrounded by some of my favorite journalists for a better reason."

Someone hooted forlornly in the audience, like a barn owl.

"When I started the Newr Report, I was very different than I am now. I was less gray." The party chuckled lightly. "I knew far less about the Internet and I hadn't had the privilege of meeting all of the great people here today. But I did know some things. I did know the power of a great story. And I had the opportunity to work with some incredible journalists to create some incredible stories. Stories that mattered. Stories that made me laugh. Stories that made me think. Especially now . . ."

The speech droned on. As it progressed, Elinor felt even sadder that the Newr Report was going under. It seemed like such an important thing now that Andrew Newr was explaining it, and Elinor almost felt ashamed. Why hadn't she read the Newr Report all the time? She had thought it was a normal website that chronicled normal things, like celebrities walking to their cars. The last story she remembered reading on it was called "10 Ways to Maximize Your Productivity Zone," which was a slide show about study habits and work productivity illustrated by luridly colored photos of a woman splayed near a computer, holding her head as if gripped by intense pain.

"It's so sad," whispered the girl Elinor was standing next to. Andrew Newr was still talking.

"I know," said Elinor. "It sucks. I read the Newr Report every day."

Elinor saw Mike silently emerging from a door underneath the Scandinavian deck. He was accompanied by a girl. They both took places near the deck to watch the progress of Andrew Newr's speech, which was still going. Mike said something in the girl's ear, and she looked at him and smiled. The girl, if Elinor remembered correctly, was named Andrea. What was Mike doing talking with Andrea? She wasn't mad, because it was a free country and Mike could talk to whomever he wanted and it was good that he had female friends, and Elinor wasn't a jealous person at all. No one had ever said to her, "You are a jealous person," ever once. She was just a person. But at the same time, how could he leave her alone all of this time? It was inhumane.

So maybe she was slightly angry and distracted when #partycat returned. She certainly wasn't looking at the cat when it eventually attached itself to her leg. She just stood there listening to the mild buzz of Andrew Newr in the background, and perhaps feeling a slight pressure on her leg if she thought about it. When she finally realized it was the cat, initially she was happy! She reached down to pet it. It was only when the cat sank its first tiny claw into her leg that she looked down and understood what was happening. That #partycat had turned against her.

At first she tried to delicately and silently jog her leg free of the cat's grip, but the cat seemed to hold on even tighter. Then it bit her in revenge for what was, in Elinor's opinion, very mild shaking. Elinor let out a small cry. Two people turned around and looked at her. In an effort to contain and modify the spectacle, she knelt down toward the cat and tried to pry it off with her fingers. But this seemed to enrage the cat even more. It sliced Elinor's neck and produced a thin scratch that immediately spouted blood. Elinor yelped and sprang up. There was excessive startling. Someone else shushed her. Andrew Newr was still talking.

"Hey, did you do something to #partycat?" a guy wearing a small and maroon sweater said as the cat slashed and slashed at her leg, and theatrically hissed, and hysterically coughed.

"No, I didn't do anything!" whispered Elinor, standing up quickly. "I absolutely did nothing to this cat." She kicked her leg then. The cat flew about three feet and landed on the Twister tarp. But the cat was fine! It immediately started running up a tree. So all the tweets about it were really uncalled for. She didn't even interrupt the speech.

. . .

Elinor and Mike left the party soon after that. On the street, it was cold. Leaves clung to the insides of gutters. The sidewalks dribbled leftover rain. It took her a while to flag a cab.

"I'm tired," Mike said, when they finally sat down in the taxi. He pressed his head into Elinor's shoulder and Elinor had a horrible desire to shrug her shoulder into his temple, but she didn't do it.

"We could've left earlier!" she said. She tried to make it sound like she was joking.

"I guess so." Mike yawned.

"You looked like you were having fun. So I didn't want to just leave or something. Even though a cat literally attacked me." Elinor looked out the window. They were pretty far away from their apartment. It was probably going to be an expensive cab fare. They should have just taken the subway.

"Well, it was okay. I don't know. It was fine, I guess."

"I saw you talking to some girl," said Elinor. "What's her name?"

"Oh, Andrea?" said Mike. "Yeah, I guess we talked." He moved his head off Elinor's shoulder and opened the window a crack. A thin stream of cold air hit her in the nose. The insides of her nostrils burned.

"You'd like Andrea a lot. She's funny. She works at Memo Points Daily."

"That's cool."

"Actually, she told me there were some open positions there. She thinks I should apply."

Elinor stretched across Mike and rolled up the window.

"I don't know if I want to work there though. You don't have a chance to write at all. I feel like you just compile political factoids into lists. Or you tweet. Can you imagine tweeting for your job? I'd fucking die."

"Yeah," said Elinor. She thought there could be worse jobs. Her job right now, for example. But that was a difference between the two of them. Mike went on and off Facebook and occasionally even read a physical paper. Elinor spent so many hours on the Internet taking quizzes, she actually felt guilty at night.

"She thinks they would like my piece on healthcare policy though. I was thinking about pitching it to them."

"Oh, really?" said Elinor. Mike had been trying to get that published for five months. It was eleven hundred words and he refused to cut any of it.

Elinor had never talked to Andrea but she had seen her around. She might have even seen her Instagram—it was appearing to her in flashes (a selfie but only of eyes, bright sun on some kind of field, a European town). Andrea was a friend of Mike's from some time in his life that he had never made entirely clear to Elinor, and she was really, really skinny. At the party, she was wearing a kind of orthopedic shoe that was probably very fashionable. Elinor had been really inappropriately dressed for this party, she realized while she was there. She wore a low-cut shirt and flesh-colored high heels that had rendered her feet blotchy and cold. At this party, everybody was wearing a black smock and wooden clogs, like they were about to attend a Dutch funeral.

"We were just talking about how dumb it all was," said Mike. "You never read long stories anymore. It's like it's dead."

"I don't know if that's true," said Elinor. "I feel like I read long stories all the time. They are so long I can't even finish them."

"You probably mean *The New Yorker*," said Mike. "That's the only magazine that publishes long stories anymore. It's like people have ADD. People have no attention spans."

"Can we just not talk about this? It's boring."

"Okay." Mike exhaled loudly. "You've been acting so weird all night."

"No, I haven't! I've been fine. I've been totally normal. I also was literally attacked by like, an animal."

"Whatever," said Mike. "If you aren't going to tell me what's wrong, then I don't even know what to say."

Elinor didn't answer him. Suddenly, she realized she was filled with rage. She started looking in her handbag, a large satchel made of plastic leather substitute. She felt around for her phone on the bottom.

"Are you going to just look at your phone now?" said Mike.

Elinor didn't say anything. She took out her phone. No one had texted her, but she looked at it anyway.

Mike hated it when she sulked. This was one of the problems they had. Mike always said that if she just told him what was wrong very clearly and rationally without getting angry, then they could resolve things. Elinor was trying to work on that. It never seemed very hard when Mike described it to her.

"I don't know," said Elinor. "I guess, I didn't really feel like you paid attention to me tonight or something. You didn't even turn around at all when I was attacked by that cat. And it really hurt me. I have a scratch on my neck! And you spent the entire time talking to Andrea. Like, at one point I looked over and she was sitting on your lap—"

"What the hell are you talking about?" said Mike. "I was literally by your side the entire night."

His voice changed. Normally, Mike spoke in a sure-footed, staccato way, but when fighting, he always initially adopted a tone that was both high and strained but ultimately surprised and incredulous. This shock always gave Elinor pause. Sometimes it made Elinor stop speaking entirely and burst into tears, merely because it could be so movingly deployed. Surprise is the most pitiable emotion—the first impulse of the falsely and abominably accused.

Then Mike pinned himself against the window of the cab, and adopted a caricature of a horrified expression—his mouth frozen in a small round O like a doll. This restored Elinor to the enjoyment of her former anger.

"That's such a fucking lie, Mike, I can't even believe you're saying it."

"You're being so fucking crazy, Elinor. You are just twisting everything around. I didn't do anything."

"Okay, well, then, I guess I should stop talking," said Elinor. "As for Andrea sitting on my lap—"

"I don't really care about that. I don't want to talk about it anymore."

"Wait, I have to explain myself, okay? Because you can't just say that I was actually like, hitting on other girls in front of you, and then be like, 'I don't care about that.' I have to explain myself. You make these ridiculous statements that have no logic and then you won't even let me explain myself."

"You really don't have to." As quickly as her temper had flared, it had also lost much of its integrity. She was tired now.

"As for Andrea sitting on my lap, she was just telling me this story about how a guy said she couldn't sit on his lap because she was too heavy. And I was like, 'That's crazy,' because you know how skinny she is, I mean, she's tiny. So she just sat on my lap, and I was like, 'That guy is crazy.' I was trying to be nice, okay? And you just took that completely out of context. Oh my *god*, Elinor," said Mike.

Elinor could see he had tears in his eyes—pinpricks of shininess in his overlarge corneas. Soon, they would plop onto his peacoat. Elinor was not shocked—as she had seen Mike cry many times in their relationship. He was probably quite drunk, but at the same time, it was possible he wasn't.

"Why are you crying?" whispered Elinor.

"I don't want you to feel bad, okay?" said Mike. He took Elinor's hand and made her look at him. Tears were all over the collar of his peacoat now. "But you're twisting everything around! I literally didn't do anything. I can't believe you're attacking me like this."

"Stop," said Elinor. Maybe she was attacking him? She didn't know what she was doing. "Don't cry, okay? I don't feel that bad. It's actually okay."

"I was not at all flirting with Andrea. I wasn't!"

"Okay. I know you weren't. But it's just really hard for me to go to a party like that. I was literally attacked by like, this crazed animal?"

"Come here," said Mike, pulling Elinor close to him so that her shoulder was jutting into the button of his peacoat. "I love you. You have to trust that I didn't mean it and I didn't do anything."

Elinor put her head on Mike's peacoat. The wool scratched her ear. Maybe the party had put her in a bad mood. Everyone was talking about getting a job or having a job and there was nothing worse.

Elinor had been in New York City for two years and four months and had not had a journalism job the entire time. She was nannying for a family. One of the children spoke only in short, high screams. Fraunces was his name. This was not what she had pictured herself doing. For as long as she could remember she had wanted to be a writer. She was actually trying to do that! It was just hard. Writing was very hard and soul crushing. Literally anyone would tell you that.

When she went to parties like these—journalism networking parties, which Mike somehow always knew about and took her to even though she wasn't invited—she felt a curious sense of impermanence, a feeling that she could dissolve into the floor. When she heard Mike say things like he wanted to write long-form reported pieces even though he was a fact-checker in his daily life, it sounded so real, such a normal thing for him to say. She didn't doubt that he would eventually do it, even. But when she tried to describe herself (a freelancer, she said), she sounded like a grifter who exaggerates her background as part of a long con. She always wished she had something better to say—a story about herself that would inspire a quick, sly look of admiration or a small uptick of respect at the end of an inquiry. So yes, parties were stressful. It would make anyone fight with anyone.

"That will be twenty-six dollars," said the cabdriver. Elinor took out a wad of bills she'd made babysitting and paid. The cabdriver was happy because it was cash.

. . .

A mere two days before this, an emergency meeting was taking place at a journalism start-up in New York City. The office was on the seventh floor of a warehouse in Soho. A hundred years ago, perhaps, this was a building where people routinely got their hair caught in a loom machine. Now there was blond wood on the floor and a bunch of temporary-looking tables with laptops on them.

Two men were sitting around one of the tables. One of them was in his early twenties. One was nearer to middle age. His hair was ash colored and long in the back. There was a web of broken capillaries covering his nose. He rubbed his temple.

"I can't believe she quit," he said. He stood up from his chair and stared at the street. "Especially in the wake of what happened."

"I know," said the twenty-something. He had an unsightly tattoo on the inside of his wrist. Otherwise, he was dressed in an oxford shirt that was buttoned all the way up to the collar. He looked both morbid and handsome, like a Victorian scientist. His name was Peter. "She said it wasn't personal."

"I know that," snapped the middle-aged man, whose name was John Wallace Thurgood. Most people called him J.W. That was his byline at his old paper. "I don't really care whether it was personal or not."

"Well, I figured you might want to know that. Because she did say that." Peter pushed his tongue against the inside of his cheek and then blew air out of his mouth. For a fundamentally serious man, he had a penchant for the theatrical, old-fashioned gesture.

J.W. returned to staring out the window. He felt panicky, which was not uncommon in his new life as the executive editor of news partnerships and media strategy at Journalism.ly. Elizabeth, a twenty-four-year-old idiot, somehow had a very important job for reasons he was unclear about. He had worked here for only six months, but even so, he had yet to understand why some jobs here were more important than other jobs. Everyone seemed like they did the same thing. They just found videos of cats rolling around on the ground or compiled lists about being an introvert. Only J.W. had to cold-call Andrew Cuomo and ask him for sponsored content (he refused).

What he did know was that Sean seemed mad that Elizabeth had quit, especially in the wake of an article called "What Journalism.ly Needs to Do to Compete in the Online World (And What It's Not Doing)," which had been published on another website called Memo Points Daily. Sean was either defiantly truculent or unaccountably wounded in the face of any online attacks, and this time, he had been very wounded. He had already written J.W. asking for a meeting to "come up with a game plan for a coordinated response to the article." Sean might even blame J.W. for what Journalism.ly needed to do and was not doing! J.W. himself had been hired in response to an article on Business Insider called "How Journalism.ly Can Live Up to Its Name (By Hiring Actual Journalists!)." He never did figure that out, however.

"Personally, I think we dodged a bullet," said Peter. "She never hacked participation. You have to hack participation. It's the currency of the Internet. I sat down with her so many times, trying to explain things."

Sometimes, J. W. would look up from his computer and stare at an unfixed point on a temporary wall, and feel like he didn't know how or why he'd ended up working at Journalism.ly. For five years he had worked at *The Village Voice,* and for fourteen normal years, he had worked at the New Jersey *Star-Ledger.* After years of being a stringer, a copy editor, a beat reporter, and a reporting editor, he finally got a job as a political reporter nine years ago. He thought he was going to do that for the rest of his life. It was a great job. The mayor called him Johnny Boy. At cocktail parties, he would regale people with stories of uncorroborated extramarital affairs between low-level staffers. At the end of his time at the *Ledger,* he was even writing a political column called "Thoughts and Musings." They gave stuff like that only to people who had really paid their dues.

Then, out of nowhere (well, out of somewhere—ads had been dwindling at the paper for years), he got laid off. He had just finished a "Thoughts and Musings" column called "Get a Life, Chris Christie." It was the last one he ever did for the paper. This was followed by twenty-two months of terrifying unemployment, in which J. W. freelanced and went to networking coffees, meet ups, and journalism conferences to try to make people remember him and offer him a job. He had the occasional conversation with an employed peer that would stanch his panic—and then his follow-up emails, though studiously casual ("Hi! Just following up on our conversation the other day") would remain ignored, and what could he do about it? Despite the fact that this era of unemployment had ostensibly ended, memories of it would sometimes engulf him while he was doing ordinary tasks, like taking dishes out of the dishwasher.

"Well, I guess we have to replace her," said J.W. wearily. "Sean apparently got a name from Pam Johnson of a girl to interview."

J.W. had gotten an email from Sean to this effect this morning—it consisted of a very long subject line with a phone number in it. Sean had a lot of very famous journalism friends, of which Pam Johnson, polemical essayist, was one. They always seemed to have more weight and influence than people who actually worked at the company, like J.W.

"We don't have very much time. Sean wants this taken care of in the next couple of weeks. Especially with the election gearing up? He's pretty upset about this," said Peter.

J.W. gave Peter a filthy look, which Peter didn't acknowledge or even seem to understand. Before this job, Peter had never written a story professionally and instead had simply impressed Sean at a student journalism conference. Very soon after that, Peter was installed as managing editor, even though usually, at the New Jersey *Star-Ledger*, for example, that took forty years. Apparently, Sean liked his "vibe" and the way he "got" social media. It wasn't, perhaps, the most stringent editing role (because no one edited anything that ever went on the site), but Peter basically oversaw operations and sometimes wrote think pieces—his own thoughts and musings! Was being a managing editor better than being an executive editor of news partnerships and media strategy? Maybe? Probably. The thought of this filled J.W. with bitterness, especially while he was doing something like asking the president of Quaker Oats to write a blog about oatmeal (he said no).

"Sean's upset?"

"Yes," said Peter, peremptorily. Peter's tenure at the company was slightly longer than J.W.'s, so sometimes he would get very strident when telling a story about an event that had happened several months previous—like only he was the keeper of history. "She was the daughter of a good friend of his. Plus she did our tweetstorms. So, it's pretty problematic."

Elizabeth was very thin and mean. She had pointy ears, a triangular chin, and a butt that looked like two tennis balls. She might have been the child of a minorly famous person, if J.W. remembered correctly. That was why she didn't care about being paid so little.

"Okay," said J.W. He had protested Twitter at first. "How can you express yourself in 140 characters?" he said in a "Thoughts and Musings" column in 2009. " 'I'm eating.' Does everyone need to know that?" In 2010, he got a Twitter account. Now he tweeted all the time. He thought he was pretty good at it. Sometimes he would make jokes. Or he would weigh in on New Jersey politics, but not too much, since that wasn't his thing anymore. Very rarely, if ever, did he get in squabbles with other journalists, but he certainly watched fights with glee and avidity.

"Well, let's get on the stick with the hiring," said J.W. "I've got a lot of work to do." He left then, even though he didn't really have anyplace to go.

. . .

A hazy light flitted through the prison bars affixed to all the windows in Elinor and Mike's apartment. It was the morning.

"El," Mike said. They were in bed together and Mike was

propped up on his cylindrical arm, checking his phone. Elinor was lying on her side and staring blankly at the table where they kept their toaster and a dirty, mustard-colored vial of salt. That was their kitchen. "You are never going to believe this."

"What?" said Elinor. Mike absentmindedly tightened his arm around her waist. Elinor felt hollow. She had been up since 4:00 a.m. thinking about how unattractive it was that she had focused much of her spooling, rather incoherent invective on Andrea, a fellow woman. It made her seem jealous when she wasn't at all. She didn't even care about Andrea. She was just drunk and stressed out about the party because they were talking about jobs there. No wonder Mike had reacted the way he had reacted. She resolved to be docile and sweet-tempered for the rest of the time.

"Andrea emailed me this morning. Apparently, she emailed her bosses and now they want me to come in for that position at Memo Points Daily?"

"Mike, what? Really?" said Elinor, who felt a strum of anxiety that Andrea had emailed Mike, and blinked very hard. She tried to blot this feeling out by turning around and burrowing her head into Mike's shoulder. Mike hugged her back while at the same time looking over her shoulder, his eyes on the harsh whiteness of his screen, which was the most piercing light source in the room (they had no lamps).

"I knew she really liked my think piece about where America's trash goes. She told me last night she always liked my writing."

"That's so great."

"I have to go in Monday. Do you think I will have time to polish up my piece this weekend?"

"Yeah, sure."

"But we have dinner with my parents tonight. Fuck."

"We can't cancel that. They scheduled it two weeks ago."

"Well, fuck, Elinor, I want to do a good job?"

"You will do a good job," said Elinor, from Mike's shoulder. "You always do."

"Fuck," said Mike. "I can't fucking believe this. Richard Cooley works at Memo Points Daily. Fuck." Richard Cooley was a former *New Yorker* reporter who'd recently left the magazine after Memo Points Daily offered him half a million dollars. He was appointed their executive supervising editor. His Twitter icon was a cartoon version of his face. In that image, he had square glasses. Elinor didn't know what he looked like in real life.

"What's the job?" she asked.

"They want a new politics guy? For the election? I think it's more of a writing position or else why would they want to see all my clips and stuff?"

Elinor got on top of Mike and kissed him on the lips. She could feel the hairs on his legs jutting into the hairs on her legs. Her legs sprouted hairs, it seemed, in the middle of the night. "Do you want to get something to eat?"

"Oh, El," said Mike. He adjusted her face downward and kissed her forehead. Elinor swallowed some of her own spit and realized it tasted like sour milk mixed with something almost chemical, like glue. She fastened her lips together in a line. She hoped Mike wouldn't be able to smell it. "I really have to get that piece in good shape. I want it to be in the best shape possible for Monday. Especially if we have to go to a dinner party at my parents' tonight."

"Okay," said Elinor. Mike had a diligence about work that intimidated her. Before they dated, she used to always see him in the library, writing on a yellow pad with a ballpoint pen, even though everyone else just used computers. "I understand."

"I love you, baby. You're so cute. You're such a cutie," said Mike in the babyish voice he sometimes used with her.

"I love you too," said Elinor. She knew this was a conclusion of their time in bed together. Mike made certain rote overtures in the prelude to hooking up (he touched her breasts, he breathed into her neck, he put his erection into her leg), and he was doing none of those things now. He was still holding his phone tightly in the other hand. Elinor kissed his neck with her pursed lips.

"I don't think she would email unless there was a very good chance, do you?"

"I don't." Mike applied a slight pressure to the left side of her body, and she dismounted to the right of him. "Do you know what the salary is?"

"I mean, I'm sure it's fine enough or else she wouldn't have emailed me," said Mike. He sounded annoyed. It didn't really matter how well it paid anyway. It was a stupid question. Mike's parents were still kind of supporting him, he made way more money than Elinor right now, and he was much better about money than she was anyway. For example, he hadn't wanted to take a cab last night. She had made them. Despite her actual lack of money, there was something in her that inexorably pushed to the mildest extravagances, like Madame Bovary. "I think it's just good experience no matter what. Wow, I've got to get going." His narrow, jointless body sat up.

Mike and Elinor lived in a basement apartment on Ninety-fourth Street and First Avenue. It didn't have a stove. They slept on a foam pad that they kept on the floor. The sheets always came off the sides of the pad, but when they'd moved here, they couldn't afford a bed and eventually it just seemed like too much of a hassle to buy one. Sometimes the pad would fold in half, almost magically, if a pillow wasn't on it.

Mike walked over to his computer, which he kept on the oblong wooden desk next to the biggest of the barred windows. He took out a stack of legal pads from a drawer underneath the desk and slammed them authoritatively on the desktop.

Elinor got up from the foam pad. She pulled the sheets over the pad in a lump and tried to make them neat in some way, but they just bunched together like pieces of lint stuck to a coat. Then she went to the table to make herself a cup of coffee. If she didn't like coffee so much, she would have thrown the coffeemaker out. It took up a lot of space.

"I heard Peter has a job," said Mike. He plopped down on his desk chair, pajama pants sagging, and started to peruse his legal pads, which were mostly blank.

"Really?" said Elinor, as she scooped coffee into the coffeemaker. Peter was Mike's sort-of friend. They had been the two top students at communications school. Elinor remembered a particular long group dinner where they had both discussed the inner workings of the communications school with a kind of byzantine shorthand that Elinor, even though she was also a student there, was at a loss to understand. Elinor didn't say much at that dinner. She remembered looking at the paper place mat on her table, which was advertising a two-for-one margarita night. That image sometimes resurfaced in her dreams. "Who told you that?"

"One of the people at the party, I forget who— Get this, he's working for Journalism.ly."

"Oh," said Elinor. "I've heard of that."

"Yeah. It's Sean Patterson's company. Tim Patterson's son?"

"I know who Tim Patterson is," said Elinor. Mike sometimes acted as if Elinor had no knowledge of journalism, which was funny because they had met in communications school, so obviously she did. "He was on *20/20* for, like, fifty years. My dad likes him."

"Jeez." Mike held up his hands.

She could tell Mike was pretending to be playfully offended but was, in actuality, offended. She continued in a lighter tone. "What about Sean Patterson?"

"I thought you knew everything about it."

"Mike," said Elinor. "I don't really. I mean, obviously you know way more about that stuff."

"Well," said Mike. He stretched out his arms. "Sean Patterson is like, some Silicon Valley venture capital guy! He wanted to start some fucking copycat of BuzzFeed that's supposed to revolutionize journalism. But it's the exact same as like, Medium. No one who matters takes it seriously. I mean, Memo Points Daily just had an amazing takedown of the whole thing on their website. I'll send it to you."

"Ugh," said Elinor. She had not heard him. In the past thirty seconds she had become engrossed in the progress of the coffeemaker. It was amazing to Elinor how one repetitive physical task could occupy almost all the space in her brain. She turned on the coffeemaker and walked to her chest of drawers. She took out the pair of pants she was going to wear today.

"I think if this trash piece is really awesome, they just might give me this job."

"Absolutely," said Elinor. "I think so too."

"I just have to keep working on it. I want to make it more about how structurally, America is incredibly irresponsible with all of its waste and how it's actually endemic of a whole host of structural problems within the society—"

"I love that. I have to go take a shower. You're going to do great. I know it."

Elinor went over to the bathtub, which was in the middle of the kitchen area. She wrapped the shower curtain around the tub, pulled a chain to unplug the drain, and turned on the water. The shower curtain was woefully inadequate. Water sprayed on the coffeemaker no matter what she did.

. . .

It was hard to say when Elinor understood that Mike was actually Mike Moriarty, the son of essayist Pam Johnson and noted First Amendment scholar Eben Moriarty. Perhaps he was pointed out at a dim, hot party or she had figured it out through the type of casual Internet stalking of strangers that was embarrassing only when you really thought about it. In any case, she knew before she met Mike that he was the son of a woman who had written essays for *Time* magazine and a man who was always on CNBC defending people whose parades were very offensive.

Mike's mother was especially famous. When Elinor was growing up, her parents had subscribed to several magazines about world affairs, and though Elinor had tried to slog through the political articles, she would always eventually flip to the back page, where Mike's mother's essay would sit, ensconced by her sober-looking picture—a woman with a bob haircut, staring dreamily into nothing. "A Mother's Guilt." "What Gen X Forgot." "Hillary's Struggle." When Elinor started to date Mike, she reread all of Mike's mother's columns online, late at night, after some stilted yet unconscionably thrilling encounter. Sometimes, during a particularly moving column about motherhood or some social problem of the nineties, she would get choked up, almost out of nerves.

All this notoriety conferred a bit of glamour on Mike at school. It probably would have eventually faded if Mike was a dull kind of person, but he wasn't. He was a "person of note" on campus. He was the editor of the alternative magazine. He was the class treasurer. He always wore a hat. In class he would get into arguments with professors that seemed remarkable for their inexplicable aggressiveness. He went to parties and invariably talked intently to the only other person in a hat there, man or woman. Everyone said he was extremely smart.

Was Elinor known for anything at college? Her mother and her father could not provide any glamour to speak of. Her best friend, Sheila, was pretty average, not famous or exciting—she used to be in the communications school but she switched out sophomore year and was now a nurse. Elinor was an excellent student—the valedictorian of her high school class, the editor in chief of her school newspaper. She oscillated between thinking she was an undiscovered gem and relatively fat. And then all of a sudden, she was dating one of the most interesting, brilliant guys at school (for a certain crowd), just by sitting with him at a Starbucks. How had she done it? In the end, it really did reflect well on her.

Elinor had been to Mike's parents' place on the Upper West Side four or five times, usually for dinner parties. Mike's dad didn't really talk, he was always "doing something on a computer" in another room, but Mike's mother was just as amazing as Elinor had thought she would be. She talked about interesting things—like abortion rights. She always served an oily, lemon-flavored roasted chicken. Elinor thought eventually they would really get along, but she couldn't quite shake the feeling that she was especially boring when she talked to Mike's mother, and that Mike's mother had noticed it. It was just that Elinor got so nervous when there was pressure on her to say something smart. And sometimes, when she had actually prepared something smart to say, as she was saying it, Mike's mother would blink and veer suddenly into unrelated conversational mores, as if she wanted Elinor to stop talking. Their relationship was simply going to take time.

At first glance, this dinner party seemed much like all the other dinner parties. There were women swaddled in knit shawls and standing in a clump next to a hulking mahogany armoire in the dining room. Mike's mother was among them. The men were in the living room, which was a separate room. Elinor was always struck by the size of Mike's parents' apartment. It was the biggest she had ever seen in New York—a living room, a dining room with a mahogany armoire *and* a table, plus two bedrooms. There was a kitchen with a prodigious amount of built-in storage that you were able to pull out of the wall using only a handlebar. Mike said it had been designed by an architect.

"Mike!" said his mother when she saw him. "You're late. Come here."

"You know I had that job thing to do," said Mike. He sounded annoyed, which was his usual tone with his mother, although when Elinor would ask about it obliquely, he never remarked on any particular grievance. Elinor filtered in behind the two of them. She tried to make a motion toward Mike's mother to greet her, but Mike's mother didn't see her because Mike's back was blocking her, so she waved unseen.

"How did it go? Mike's applying for this job at Memo Points Daily," she told the group. The group made various gestures of understanding (nodding, blinking, smiling).

"I think my daughter has a friend who works there," said one of the women. She was wearing red glasses.

"Did you end up redoing the waste treatment piece?" asked Mike's mother.

"Of course I did," said Mike.

"Did you add the part I wanted you to add?"

"I don't know. I added a lot to the second section."

"What did you add?"

"Well, I ended up cutting the thing about the mayor's role."

"Did you at least call that woman? Cathy Presoni? She could have helped you with that. I told her you were going to call her."

"Yes, I called her. But she wasn't that helpful."

"What did you ask her?"

"Mom, what the fuck is wrong with you? I just got here. Where's the wine?"

"There's wine in the living room with your father."

"Okay," said Mike. He wriggled out of his mother's grasp and stomped toward the living room. Elinor didn't know what to do. Should she follow him? Or would that seem antisocial, because she was also a woman and should stay with the women? She decided to stay where she was.

"That's great about the job, Pam. Ethan is still an intern. Even though he's been working there for like, five months for free," said one of the other women.

"It's horrible," said the woman with red glasses. "I mean, we didn't even have internships when I was coming up. It's robbery. And it's robbery of us. Because we're the ones that have to pay for it."

"I mean, look at Mike. He's such a gifted writer and he's just such a hard worker," said Mike's mother. "He was the most like me of any of the kids. His sister I have to *beg* to do anything. I told him, don't settle. Don't get a reporting job until it's really a reporting job. I mean, he has a job now, but you know, a real job, where he gets to write. And honestly, even for *him* it has been harder than I think it should be. Things really need to change in this country. Now."

"We need a revolution. I've been saying that."

"Can you call anyone?" said the woman with red glasses. She was drinking red wine and some of it had settled on her upper two teeth, like fog over a pond.

"I have a friend, Maureen O'Donnaugh. She worked with me at the magazine. I was going to call her on Monday."

Mike's mother had been fired during the financial crisis and now enjoyed a successful freelance career. She had recently written a column called "Marriage Is Marriage" for *The New*

York Times's "Modern Love" column. Elinor had put it on her Facebook wall. Mike's mother was her friend. But Mike's mother didn't like it or anything.

"You should call her," said the woman who had smiled at Elinor. She had a suspiciously lineless and shiny chin. "Isabella is interning at that nonprofit theater troupe I told you about, but it's only because I called up Carol Sargent and begged her."

"Oh, I'm going to," said Mike's mother. "But I don't know if it will do any good."

"They say the economy is recovered, but honestly, I don't know how that can be."

"Did you read that article in *The New Yorker* about real wages? It's absolutely not recovered."

"And I mean, of course you can see it in all swaths of life, the disappearance of the country's safety net. It's absolutely systemic. And you can see it because these kids are having the toughest time finding jobs. I mean, look at Mike—look at Isabella."

"Look at Ethan," said Red Glasses, in an offended way, about Ethan.

"And if these kids can't get jobs, I mean, who can?" said Mike's mother. She shook her head. "Mike won every prize you could get in school when he graduated. I mean, he really is the most brilliant kid. I know I'm his mother, but I feel like I can say objectively—"

"And what do you do, honey?" said the Chin. Elinor had no idea she was doing it, but she was making a very pained-looking face. When addressed, Elinor felt keenly the social relief of being able to say something and simultaneous pressure for it to be an utterance of quality.

"Me?" she said. "I'm trying to be a journalist too." She cleared her throat.

"And guess what?" said Mike's mother. "She's been baby-sitting this whole time. And didn't you graduate nearly the top of your class too?"

Elinor felt a rush of gratefulness toward both Mike (in the other room still, she could see his wasted back through the doorway) and his mother. When had Mike told his mother that she had graduated at the top of her class? Maybe she had told Mike's mother the last time she came here actually. In any case, she was glad that Mike's mother knew that about her. And it was so nice of her to mention it!

"You know," said the woman in the turtleneck to Elinor. "I just ran into Jane, Jane Targson? Out to coffee the other day. She can be, well, hard is an understatement, she's kind of a bitch, but she'd be a great person to informationally interview. I don't even know what she's doing now after that thing at the *Times,* but just to get an idea of how kind of—"

"I'm sure I could help you," said Mike's mother. "Heck, I've worked most places in this city. You don't even know the jobs I did. I was Gary Sassoon's assistant and he was a total pervert."

"Oh my god, that would be amazing," said Elinor.

"It's so different though, now," said Red Glasses. "When I was working at Condé Nast, we took town cars home every night. We didn't know how good we had it."

"We absolutely didn't. The book leave I used to get?"

"Don't even talk about it," said the Chin. "Everything is so different now."

"Oh, you know who's hiring?" said Mike's mother. "Journalism.ly. Tim Patterson was telling me about it. You know, his son runs it? Apparently his son was very upset about that takedown in Memo Points Daily, and wants to invest more in investigative journalism or something? So that could be interesting. I told him I knew people. I'll mention you."

"You would do that?" squeaked Elinor.

"I see him every Sunday at this board we're both on. He's the only non–hedge funder on the whole thing, so I have to talk to him. This board is so obnoxious, I don't know why I do it. I mean, I know why I do it, it's because I believe in the charity, but—"

"That would be so helpful," said Elinor.

A thought passed through Elinor's mind, unwanted and dreadful—did Mike's mother share Mike's disparagement of Journalism.ly and therefore her suggestion of Elinor for that particular job was some kind of subterranean neg? Then, however, she dismissed it. There was no way Mike's mother could do that. It was not what she wanted to think.

An important fact about Elinor that the reader should know is that even though she often felt a lot of free-floating, nonspecific anxiety, she was actually very good at blocking out specific thoughts. Here's how it worked: An anxiety-provoking thought would surface, unbidden, in her mind, but almost as soon as it happened, a new thought would occur in its place. The new thought usually adopted the kind of positivist, instructive, and generalized tone of the personal essays Elinor read on the Internet, which gave Elinor a feeling that the new thought was better than the old thought because it was valorized by collective wisdom. Instead of worrying about Mike's mother, and her specific idiosyncrasies or motivations, for example, Elinor would start to think about mothers in general, and how they loved their children but needed individuality. This new thought would then compete with the latent anxiety left behind by the old thought, the content of which Elinor had almost convinced herself she had forgotten.

Mike came back with a glass of wine then. He had one glass in each hand. Elinor beamed at him. She loved him so much all of a sudden, his lopsided hair, the virulent tone he always used with his mother. He had even gotten her a glass of wine without asking, which was such a nice thing to do.

The rest of the dinner went on as usual. Mike talked to his mother and her friends about current events. Elinor tried to chime in—sometimes she sounded banal and sometimes she sounded slightly garbled. For once she didn't care. She also got a bit too drunk at dinner, but everyone sort of did.

Chapter 2

Facebook: 1 status update: "I've got a big job interview this week and I have a question since I haven't done this in a while. Do you really have to print your resume out anymore? Can't everyone pull it up on their phones?" Four likes, two comments. Comment 1, a friend from college: "Congrats on the job interview!" Comment 2, a friend of Elinor's mother and a heavy Facebook user: "You don't have to print out your resume, but I do think it's a nice gesture."

Twitter: 15 tweets, slightly more journalistically inflected than usual. Perhaps Elinor thought her future employers would be looking at her Twitter. Sample: "Thought-provoking article about waste treatment from @Mike_Moriarty_Journo. We need to know where our trash goes! #knowyourtrash."

Instagram: 2 pictures. Picture 1: Elinor's street taken from the top of her roof. It's not a very beautiful vista, but it is dense. There is a series of ruddy tenements and the occasional brutalist apartment building. The trees look desiccated. Caption: "First time up on my roof this year. #pretty #NYCwinter #WinterIsComing."

Picture 2: Mike and Elinor. It is from when they were in college, which you can tell from the lack of ostensible filter, Elinor's American Apparel leotard, and Mike's hat. In the picture, Elinor is kissing Mike on the cheek. He is blinking. Caption: "To my amazingly sweet, funny, kind boyfriend. Thank you for always getting me pizza at 3 in the morning, just because 'I need it.' Thank you for helping me cope with work and for letting me complain endlessly about my stress even when you have your own shit to do. And thank you for doing the dishes last night. Here's to another year with my best friend."

. . .

E linor talked to Mike for the first time in October of senior year. Elinor was sitting in Starbucks, in a sweater that was always a little too wide, drinking a cinnamon sugar latte. She was studying for her History of Communications class and feeling guilty about the latte. Elinor loved food, and she was also a distracted, impulsive, and tetchy eater. While studying, she could eat an entire bag of Rold Gold pretzels like it was a pack of gum. She realized she wasn't horribly fat, but she was in no way skinny either. At a certain point the year before, she'd realized she was developing an immutable second roll on her stomach.

Mike walked up to her table. There was an empty seat in front of her and he put his bag on it.

"Do you mind if I sit here?" he said. Elinor was a little surprised. She knew who Mike was, but they had never talked before.

"Of course," said Elinor. "I'm Elinor by the way."

"Mike." Mike held out his hand. Elinor shook it, and Mike gave her a lugubrious smile. Then he went into his leather rucksack and took out a stack of legal notepads and laid them on the table. He also took out his History of Communications textbook and placed it carefully next to the notepads.

"You're studying for History of Communications?" said Elinor. "Me too!" She held up her book.

"Cool," said Mike.

"You know, I think I've seen you around before." Elinor realized then she was not going to bother anymore with the pretense that she didn't know who he was. People did that, but personally, she always felt like it was a little bit rude, or hypocritical or something.

"What year are you?" asked Mike.

"I'm a senior."

"Me too! How come I don't know you?"

"I don't know!"

Mike chuckled.

"I like your honesty. Everyone else I have ever met would have acted like they didn't actually know me but secretly they would have known me? I love that you didn't do that. It's so fucking shitty."

"Oh thanks," said Elinor. She became red. "Yeah, that's so dumb."

"Where do you think you have seen me?" he asked her, looking at her in an unblinking way. "I want to know."

"I don't know—around, I guess," said Elinor, feeling a little uncomfortable. "We take this class together so maybe that's it."

"Oh yeah," said Mike, looking, Elinor thought, slightly disappointed. He took off his hat and ran his fingers through his hair. He had sweat into the front of the hat slightly, but Elinor still thought he was handsome. He had small, determined features and well-cut clothing. Plus, she thought writing things on legal pads was kind of cool. Elinor just took notes on her laptop. "Do you like the class?"

"It's okay. Do you?"

"The professor's a fucking idiot."

"Yeah," Elinor agreed. When she thought about it, she didn't like him much either. He spat when he talked. There were so many lectures about the female reporter who had dressed up like a mental patient and hid in a mental hospital and won a prize. Elinor had forgotten her name. She knew she was right about thinking this class was so boring. Elinor's father said she often said things were boring when she didn't understand them enough. That was why he made her go on the high school debate team, the biggest disaster of her life.

"I'm so glad you said that! I thought I was going nuts. Everyone likes him, even though he's fucking crazy. There was this amazing infographic on Think Lab the other day that completely rebutted his lecture on Tuesday. I'll send it to you, but essentially, it just traces the way freedom of the press evolved throughout history and how it's contracting. It's truly scary."

"Wow," said Elinor. Mike seemed very serious, and Elinor was rather impressed. She wished she sounded like that— finding granular information on Think Lab, a site she had only vaguely heard of, and then recalling it, as if it had somehow become part of her marrow. She studied and got good grades, but that was mere application. This guy sounded like he was really brilliant. "That's so cool."

"I kind of hate the Internet too," said Mike. "Like, I go on and off Facebook. I'm not on Instagram. But I do read Think Lab."

"I've totally heard of Think Lab."

"I bet you love the Internet. I bet you're always on Instagram. Hashtagging your pumpkin spice latte or something?"

"Ha-ha," said Elinor, stung. Did she look really lame? Was that so lame to do, anyway? Because she had actually Instagrammed a latte, but like, two years ago, before it was a thing. And so many people she knew still did it. At least she wasn't still doing it! "No way. I mean, I have an Instagram, but everyone does."

"I bet it's all lattes. Let me look at your Instagram."

"No," said Elinor. "Besides, you don't even know my name. And I'm private. Maybe I won't confirm you."

"I'll figure it out," said Mike, smiling at her.

It was at this point that Elinor realized Mike was really different from any guy she had known before. For example, in her sophomore year, she'd dated one of the guys who lived below her in her apartment building. He was small and wore large shirts. He was friends with all the guys downstairs, but in the particular way men have, his roommates always treated him with a benign tolerance and no real affinity, sort of like he had always been invited at the last minute to fill in for someone else. He laughed very eagerly at most jokes and loved to play video games. They dated for only three months and they didn't even break up. They just stopped hooking up one day like they had forgotten about each other. Mike could feel a surging, moralistic passion without humiliation. He could rescue her from her most potent fears about herself—the banality that she sometimes worried didn't even have the virtue of a particular visual idiom. This is what Elinor desperately craved even though she wouldn't have put it quite like that.

Mike and Elinor studied next to each other for the next two hours. At the end of it, Mike stood up and yawned.

"Well, I need to go to a meeting at the *Quill*," he said. The *Quill* was the alternative magazine on campus. Mike, she vaguely remembered, was an editor there or something? She had tried to get on it her freshman year and they had rejected her. It wasn't a big deal though; it was a very competitive process.

"Can I get your number though?"

"My number?" said Elinor.

"If you want to go over any of this stuff."

"Okay," said Elinor. She tried to hide her shock. He wanted to talk to her more about what stuff? She told him her number.

"I'll text you," said Mike. He put his hat back on his head, stuffed his notepads back into his rucksack, and walked out of the Starbucks.

. . .

"What did you end up doing on Friday?" asked Sheila. They were sitting in Sheila's apartment watching some version of the *Housewives* franchise on a laptop with a plastic keyboard protector on top of it. Elinor had a fleece blanket wrapped in a complicated fashion around her legs. Sheila sat to the side of her in a hooded sweatshirt. There was a dark gray cast in the apartment, despite the fact that it was only 3:00 p.m. Pustules of water were clinging to the oblong windows of Sheila's living room.

"Friday sucked. Well, it was sort of okay," said Elinor. "Mike and I got in a kind of a fight."

"Oh no!" Sheila plucked at her scrubs pants. On Tuesdays, Sheila worked mornings. This Tuesday, Elinor had gotten the afternoon off because Ramona was sick and her mother had decided to stay home with her.

"Yeah, we went to that party in Greenpoint."

"I would've gone to that but I was fucking exhausted. What did you wear?"

"That green shirt thing."

"I love that."

"Do you think it's cute? I feel like it makes me look fat."

"No, it's so cute."

"Anyway," said Elinor. She never really trusted Sheila's sense of style. "I felt like Mike was ignoring me and I kind of yelled at him on the way home in the cab."

"What did he do?"

"Well, I don't know. I could have overreacted? A girl sat on his lap."

"What the fuck? Were you pissed? I would have been so pissed."

"It wasn't that big of a deal," said Elinor, irritated, though Sheila was agreeing with her. "He didn't mean it. It was a joke or something."

"Oh, okay."

"I think I just misinterpreted it. He actually cried he felt so bad."

"He cried?" said Sheila. "I don't think I've ever seen Ralph cry, like ever." Ralph was a guy Sheila had been in love with since they were eighteen years old. She had sex with him approximately six times a year and yet they still managed to have a dramatic relationship. Sheila was always yelling at

Ralph in a large party full of strangers. Ralph was always text-ing Sheila at 3:00 a.m. with the word "Hey" but nothing else. He would date other women occasionally, and Sheila would look at those women on Facebook and Instagram and generate virulent insults about them that still managed to shock Elinor when she thought about them later.

"But I don't know, I think I just felt bad because I didn't know anyone at the party," said Elinor. "I probably shouldn't have yelled at him."

"I think Mike's just so sensitive," said Sheila. "It's kind of adorable." When Sheila was in the communications school, she, at some point, had had a class with Mike. Ever since Eli-nor and Mike had started dating, in Elinor's opinion, Sheila had seemed to appoint herself some kind of Mike expert, and Elinor had to work, constantly and without rest, to disabuse her of this notion.

"I don't want to be a nagging girlfriend," said Elinor, to close the subject with some finality.

"You're not," said Sheila. "I bet he's just stressed out because of his job situation."

"Well, Memo Points Daily called him in for an interview on Monday."

"Oh my god! That's cool. What will he do?"

"It's a good job, I think? Mike says they will let him write. He has that fact-checking job but he hates it."

"That's cool," said Sheila. They started watching *Housewives* in silence.

"Lisa Rinna is such a bitch," said Sheila.

"I like her," said Elinor. "It's Kim that's the bitch."

"Kim's more crazy."

"But she's also super bitchy."

Kim was acting very drunk at a brunch and telling everyone they weren't being supportive. Elinor and Sheila watched the scene together for a while.

"Did I tell you that Ralph just told me that he's not coming to the party I'm having, and it's my fucking birthday. You're so lucky Mike's not doing shit like that."

"That's true," said Elinor. And she really was. "I wish I was less of a bitch."

"You're not a bitch."

"Ha-ha," said Elinor, not really laughing. She left fifteen minutes later. Both parties felt traumatized in a vague way. That was how they usually felt after a long, aimless period hanging out together. Still, they were best friends.

. . .

On the way back home, Elinor texted Mike about dinner. Mike took a full fifteen minutes to respond. "I was just going to get a piece of pizza. I'm at a coffee shop now #werking on my thing." Then he sent an emoji of a pizza slice.

Elinor texted back that that was fine, although for some reason she couldn't name, Mike's tone in this missive made her nervous. Sometimes, she would sense imperceptible swings in Mike's mood from very mundane-seeming text messages. This one, for example, included no particular endearments or invitation to get pizza with him. She could invite herself, of course, but would that make him think she wasn't letting him work?

This was when she realized she had a missed call and a voice mail from a nonspecific Manhattan number. She wondered if it was her student loan, who was always calling her from different areas of the country like a well-traveled spy.

"Hello," an older man's voice said doubtfully into the phone. "It's J. W. Thurgood, um, John Wallace Thurgood from the Journalism.ly. We got your name from Pam Johnson. Anyway, we want to interview you for an exciting new position at the Journalism.ly. Can you send your résumé, clips, et cetera to JW@journalismly.com and we can set you up for an interview in the next few weeks? Thanks for your time and we look forward to hearing from you."

Chapter 3

Facebook: 1 post: "Congratulations to Mike Moriarty [hyper-linked] who just got a job at Memo Points Daily!!!!!! I'm so proud of my brilliant, supportive, creative boyfriend. You are such an inspiration to me. I can't wait to see what you are going to write! ;)" Ninety likes. They had a lot of overlapping friends, and Mike was off Facebook again.

Twitter: 20 tweets. Lots of quotes again. Sample: "Nothing worth doing doesn't cause anxiety and pain in equal measure. —Anonymous." Favorited two times, both times by eggs.

Instagram: 1 picture. Of the former factory building in Soho that now houses Journalism.ly. The edifice is late Victorian and decorated by imposing filagree rendered in stone. The photographer (Elinor) must have been across the street while taking the picture as a taxicab sped in front of the building. It gives the whole thing a rather romantic, metropolitan effect. Caption: "Today's the day! Wish me luck!" Twenty-two likes. Two comments. One from Sheila—"Good luck gurrrrl! You are going to kill it!!!" Another from Elinor's brother's wife, a spiritual woman who often posts unflattering pictures of her child: "Wishing you all good things!!"

. . .

Elinor was sitting on a white fiberglass chair in a windowless reception area that did not seem to contain a receptionist. She was wearing a navy-blue pencil skirt. The skirt was a shade too tight. It kept bunching up around Elinor's hips whenever she sat down, like the skin of a snake.

Five minutes beforehand, Elinor had rung a plastic doorbell that was delicately mounted next to a pair of frosted-glass double doors. The doors had the words "The Journalism.ly" written on them in *New York Times* lettering. After a certain amount of time, a pudgy man wearing eyeliner had answered the door and told her to sit on this fiberglass chair. So now she was sitting on it.

One nerve-racking aspect of this whole affair was that she still didn't quite know what she was interviewing for. On the phone to set up an interview time, that guy who called her, a man named J.W., hadn't offered too much about the position except she had to "know Twitter and be on the forefront of technology and reporting and have innovative ideas about it." Elinor thought she could handle that. She even had her résumé printed out.

In a room just beyond the reception area, J.W. was pouring himself a cup of coffee. The coffee looked like oil and had tiny grounds floating in it. The coffeemaker had been broken for months. Sometimes, it would just spit grounds into a cup and not even coffee. He sipped it gingerly.

"A girl is here!" an employee yelled at J.W., who spilled his coffee a little.

"Who?" said J.W. He patted his tie. He was happy to note he had not spilled any coffee on it.

"She says she's here for a job interview?" said the employee. J.W. didn't know this employee's name, but he seemed as terrible as all the others. He was wearing eyeliner and a cream-colored T-shirt advertising what looked to be a very violent band. "She's here. She's outside."

"Oh yeah?" said J.W. He had forgotten about this. He was supposed to be on a call with the Orange Growers Association of America, asking them to write a blog called "10 Reasons Why Vitamin C Is Secretly Awesome," but that could wait until the end of the day, he supposed.

"Do you want me to show her into the conference room?"

"Absolutely," said J.W.

J.W. was sometimes embarrassed that he didn't have an office to himself (at the New Jersey *Star-Ledger* he'd had an office with a brown microsuede couch in it), but to be fair, no one at the company did. It was an "open-plan" office. If you wanted to have a one-on-one meeting or something, like when Elizabeth quit because she needed "time to herself" (even though she was twenty-two fucking years old so J.W. didn't even know what that meant), you could use a tiny conference room encased in glass. J.W. walked over and sat down at the table in the conference room. A couple of minutes later a girl came and plopped herself down at the table next to J.W. She had the globular eyes of a 1920s movie star.

"Hi," said J.W. He smiled. "Welcome to the Journalism.ly. I'm John Wallace Thurgood."

"Thanks so much for having me," said Elinor in a very fake-sounding voice. She felt like vomiting. All week she had been paralyzed by an abject terror. When Ramona bit Fraunces at the playground on Wednesday, she had stared at both of them blankly until they started crying in unison. The worries had oscillated. Sometimes, she would wonder how embarrassed Mike's mother would be if she didn't actually get this job that she had put her up for, and then sometimes, she would think, Is this job good enough? And which was worse? Last night, she had made Mike run through practice interview questions with her.

"What questions did they ask you in your interview?" she kept asking him, from a prone position on the foam pad, her arm draped over her forehead. "I doubt they will ask you the same questions," said Mike, annoyed. "It's a very different kind of place." Then Elinor had cried: "Do you think Journalism.ly is worse than Memo Points Daily?" Mike had told her she was being illogical.

"Here's my résumé," said Elinor. She passed it to John Wallace Thurgood across the table. He took it and read it.

"You're from Chicago?" said John Wallace Thurgood.

"Yes," said Elinor. "Outside it."

"How did you like it there?"

"It's great."

"Yeah. It's a great place."

They paused and looked at each other. Elinor smiled and then pulled down her skirt.

"I think someone's knocking on the door."

Elinor saw Peter, Peter from school, knocking on the glass door in front of them very insistently. Earlier this week, Elinor had wondered whether it was more politically expedient to email Peter before her interview to kind of "touch base" with him or whether it was better to just say hi to him once she got into the building. She didn't really know him well enough to email him (and she didn't have his email) so she eventually decided against emailing. Now that she saw Peter's dilated pupils through the glass wall, she wondered if she had made a mistake. Was Peter coming in to say hello to her? Was he mad she had not emailed? The last time she saw him, she was walking down the street in front of the communications building with Mike, and Peter said hello only to Mike. They talked for a long time in front of her about jobs they were going to have after school was over. Then they said their goodbyes.

"You can meet our managing editor," said J.W. He made some ostensibly welcoming motion to Peter, and Peter opened the door and sat down. Elinor couldn't believe Peter was in such a position of power. Managing editor? (Everyone at the Journalism.ly had extremely august titles. If you were there for six months, you could become a vice president.)

"Hi, Peter!" said Elinor, brightly. "Good to see you again."

"Uh, hi," said Peter gruffly. Elinor noticed he had changed his style since arriving in New York City. Back at college, he used to wear only polo shirts and sweatshirts that advertised their school in white block letters. But now he was wearing a button-down shirt with the collar fastened tightly into his neck. Elinor regretted again her choice of skirt. It probably made her look too traditional, not particularly cool. She should have gone with those old-people shoes that everyone was wearing at that party. But where did they get them? Elinor hadn't seen them in a store. Maybe they were at a thrift store.

"Do you two know each other?" said John Wallace Thurgood.

"Peter and I went to school together," said Elinor. "I was going to email you that I was interviewing here, but I didn't have your address." She smiled at Peter. "I was going to Facebook message you I mean. I'm sorry."

"Oh?" said Peter. He looked blank. "Really? Maybe. I'm sorry. I don't—"

"I was in a class with you. I went to college with you. You know—Mike Moriarty?" Was it possible that Peter didn't remember her? They had run into each other what seemed to have been millions of times. They'd taken a class together. They had had a boring and terrible dinner in a small group. She was pretty sure she was his Facebook friend. Maybe she wasn't—she would check when she left. And yet, maybe he legitimately had forgotten her? It could explain how many times he had spoken to Mike and not to her even though she was also there, just smiling at both of them.

"Oh," said Peter, looking at the wall behind Elinor. "Mike Moriarty. I definitely know him. Well, cool, good to see you again." He gave Elinor a wan smile. "I'm just stepping in because J.W. and I had talked earlier about me sitting in on all of the interviews because it's important for my job as managing editor, so I was worried this interview had started without me."

"We're just getting started now," said J.W. He remembered when Peter had said that he wanted to sit in on interviews. He just hated it. J.W. crossed his leg in Elinor's direction in order to signal the end of the conversation. "How did you like school?"

"I liked it a lot!" said Elinor. She shook her head a little to try to clear it. "It was really interesting to be at school during the rise of social media and how it changed journalism. Now journalism is so much more interactive. We're reporting stories in a totally new way. I'm really interested in the intersection between more user-generated content and reporter-driven content."

Elinor was trying to keep her mind on what she was saying, but she was distracted by increasingly incensed internal questions that had no answers. How dare Peter pretend not to know her! Did he make her look like she was making up the fact that she knew him in front of J.W.? What if someone told Mike's mother that she had pretended to know someone? Did Peter know Mike's mom?

"You know, I was in newspapers before," said J.W. "And what I like about Journalism.ly is that we really care about journalism. We're reporters."

"Oh yes," said Elinor. "That's really great."

"It says here," said J.W., looking at her résumé again, "that you took an investigative reporting seminar with James Fennimore. How was that?"

"Yes!" said Elinor. "Well, it was actually really interest—"

"I think we need to qualify what we mean by 'reporting,'" said Peter, who seemed to have expanded somehow, like a plastic toy you put in water overnight. His elbows were spread two feet apart. J.W. barely had any space anymore. "Especially in the context of this election! The job of viral trends editor is a lot. It means we are going to need someone who has a revolutionary understanding of how things go viral, and also how to stay true to the Journalism.ly mission. Your job would be really important to that."

"Definitely," said Elinor. "I actually once wrote a piece in college that—"

"Because I think another thing that we stand for is fairness and accuracy," said Peter. "We don't put up stuff just because it's viral, like Memo Points Daily said we did."

"I was just going to say that," said J.W. quickly. He didn't know where these kids got their fucking confidence. "You can't report something just because it's on Twitter."

"Exactly," said Elinor. "I believe that too!"

"This is a good example. Our politics editor, Josh?" Peter thrust one of his elbows in the direction of the newsroom, perhaps at Josh. "Josh just put together something that I thought was so impactful. 'The Nine Greatest Insults from the Republican Debate.' He went on CNN about it."

"Oh good," said Elinor.

Elinor wondered if anyone in the newsroom could hear her through these glass walls. Sometimes people in the main room would occasionally fixate on her like they were watching her progress and hating what she was saying. How much did glass insulate one from sound?

Elinor knew now that things were going terribly. She knew that she wasn't really answering questions—but she also didn't know what she could have said that would have made things proceed differently. The whole thing reminded her of when she was on the debate team in high school. Elinor's father had made her try out because he wanted her to learn how to think on her feet. First they were given a topic. It was like "Should people eat as much unhealthy food as they want?" and you had to argue both sides. The whole time, Elinor felt like she had opinions about things but everything she wanted to say was so distorted yet strangely emotional she couldn't even say it. After a while, she just wanted to scream, "Who cares? No one knows that answer!" But that was the thing about a debate. You had to actually pretend like you cared about something that had no answer.

"I completely agree that you can't just report things because they are on Twitter. I think the Internet has sped things up, but it has also made the tenets of investigative reporting even more important, really."

"I agree," said J.W., though he didn't seem very interested. "Well, we will definitely let you know about the job. We'll walk you out."

J.W. and Peter led Elinor out to the reception area. Other employees, many in flannel shirts of varying color and quality, gawped at her as she walked down the hall. Elinor felt sick. She tried to walk as far away from Peter as possible and positioned herself all the way on the other side of J.W., even though he kept slowing down and speeding up inconveniently, as if he were riding a Segway.

"Well, it was really nice meeting you," said J.W.

Peter shook her hand. He didn't look at her face.

"It was really nice meeting you!" said Elinor to the group of them. The fake voice had returned.

"We'll be in touch next week," said J.W.

"Okay," said Elinor, despondently. "Well, I really had a lot of fun." She walked sadly down the stairs, checking her phone.

. . .

"Well," said Peter. "What did you think of her?" Peter had followed J.W. into the kitchen—a grimy cubby with neon track lighting. In many ways, it was J.W.'s favorite place in the entire office because it had walls. J.W. poured himself another cup of coffee. He didn't speak right away.

"I thought she was good," said Peter. "I think she has a good understanding of the social landscape." A salient fact about Peter that is pertinent to this story is that he had no idea J.W. hated him as much as he did. He thought they got along great. He thought J.W. probably forgot to invite him to this interview with Elinor because it happened to slip his mind.

J.W. nodded, ruminatively, but still didn't speak, now out of pride. To be honest, he didn't really care either way. What did anyone do here anyway? Elinor had graduated from college. She came recommended from Pam Johnson of all people. She could probably tweet and Snapchat and Instagram and make listicles and write personal essays.

"Peter, come here!" said a girl who had just run into the kitchen. "We tweeted about Julia Roberts's charity and we spelled it wrong and now she's threatening to sue us and Sean is *so* mad!"

"Oh god," said Peter. "We've got to set up a process that controls this! I want to automate it—if someone tries to sue us we just automatically deal with it. It's not a good use of our time!" And he ran in the direction of the girl's computer.

J.W. watched Peter sprint into the open-plan office, a flurry of concern. This kid was telling J.W. who to hire? Who the fuck did he think he was? But then J.W. was reminded of something he had realized, to varying degrees, many times before—Peter technically outranked him. The situation, in all of its disregard of time and progress, still rankled.

J.W. finished his coffee and put the cup in the sink. Then

he marched to the conference room he had just been in and prepared to work there for the rest of the day. He was going to hire her, he decided. But it annoyed him.

. . .

Elinor was buying a black and white cookie at Dean & DeLuca. She was depressed.

"That will be three nineteen," said the woman working behind the counter. She gave Elinor the cookie. She was wearing the chef costume they made the employees wear. She looked tired.

"Oh, can I have a latte too? A large caramel latte," said Elinor.

"I'll have to ring you up separately for that," said the woman. "Because I already rang this up." She pointed at the cookie.

"I'm really sorry," said Elinor.

The woman didn't say anything and proceeded to ring up the latte.

Her phone rang, and it was Mike. Elinor picked up, and nudged the phone between her shoulder and her ear.

"Elinor, you are never going to believe this," he yelled into the phone. It sounded like he was in a bar. Elinor could hear the faint echo of Bruce Springsteen and screaming in the background. "I got it. I got the job."

"Mike! That's amazing!" said Elinor. She took a bite of her cookie. Then she paid six more dollars to the cashier for her latte.

"Andrea told me. I guess they really liked me in the interview."

"Who are you out celebrating with?" said Elinor. She mouthed "Thank you" to the cashier and took her latte off the coffee bar.

"Oh, Andrea and a couple of other people. Come if you want to."

"Well, where are you guys?" asked Elinor.

"We're at Botanica."

Elinor had been to Botanica a couple of times—very drunk. She had a memory of hitting the corner of a table with her hip there. It was rather close by.

"Well, I'm actually near there."

"Oh right!" said Mike. "The interview. Your interview. How did it go?"

"Oh I don't know. I couldn't tell."

"I bet you did great."

"No I didn't."

"Well, even if you didn't," said Mike, "it's not a big deal."

"Peter was there? He actually acted like he didn't know me, which was so bizarre because I have met him a million times—"

"El, just tell me when you get here because it's kind of loud in here. Or text me."

"I'll be there in five minutes," said Elinor. She took a sip of her latte and left Dean & DeLuca. The latte wasn't even good—it tasted scorched, like the coffee had calcified in the pot. Elinor threw it out on the street into a perforated metal wastebasket overflowing with trash.

It didn't necessarily surprise Elinor that Mike had gotten the job. He was the type of guy who always got things. At the end of college, he got like, five book awards.

Elinor arrived at the entrance of Botanica in seven minutes.

She walked down the stairs to the bar, which was very crowded, dark, and artificially cold like a cave. After a brief scan of the room, she couldn't see Mike anywhere so she went up to the bar, ordered herself a four-dollar beer, and tried to look for him. She knew she looked stupid, wandering around with her phone in her hand, peering over the tops of heads. Eventually, she found him in the back at a table with Andrea and a couple of other people Elinor had never seen before—a disastrously pale man with glasses and a girl with sloping shoulders wearing a commodious jean jacket.

"Hey," said Elinor.

"El!" said Mike. He waved from the table, but didn't get up. He was sitting next to Andrea, so Elinor sat on his other side, near the other two people.

"So, I just got us another round of shots," said Andrea to the whole table, perhaps to welcome Elinor. She pointed to a collection of thimble-size plastic cups filled with what looked like jaundiced water. They were all collected in the middle of the table. Elinor didn't think that Andrea, who looked a bit like Virginia Woolf, was the type of woman who would just buy a round of shots for a table, but Elinor was wrong. Elinor always associated high spirits with fleshy types. It was a cognitive bias that she had.

"And I think we should all take them at the same time. Like it's college or something."

"Because it kind of *is*," said Mike. "You know? Even though we're twenty-six."

"Hahahahaha, definitely," said Andrea. "This is like, such a squad goals moment. Even though I hate that squad. I mean, they are so stupid. Yet, I feel like it's appropriate. #squadgoals. LOL."

The shots were all pushed in various directions on the table, and each person took the one closest to them. Elinor downed hers quickly. It was tequila, and it tasted like vomit all the way down the back of her throat.

"Have you heard you can make synthetic diamonds with tequila?" Mike said.

"No," said Andrea. "That's fascinating."

"They can," said Mike. "I just read an article about it."

"Hahahahahaha," said Andrea. "You should tweet that, loser." But she said it in a gamine sort of way.

"Oh god." Mike laughed. "Speaking of fucking Twitter. I couldn't believe that fight that Harry Martinson got in with Richard Cooley today about the debate? It makes me want to go off Twitter. I can't take the ridiculousness."

"The debate was ridiculous though," said Andrea.

"True," said Mike, taking a swig of his beer. "They are all such clowns."

"And if they aren't clowns, they are so corrupt," said Andrea, in a solemn way.

"True," said Mike.

"Cheers," said the very pale one, who was now revealed to be British. "Cheers to Mike! On this new job!"

"Cheers," everyone said, and they all clinked glasses together.

At this point, Elinor decided to go to the bathroom. Once she got into the bathroom, she stood there and looked in the mirror. She looked much worse than she had at the beginning of college, she thought. She was fatter by ten pounds and she was getting a wrinkle in the middle of her forehead that seemed to be deadening into a permanent furrow. Maybe that was why Peter didn't recognize her. She fished a mauve-colored lip gloss out of her bag and applied it carefully to her lips. The tube was covered with some kind of black goop—perhaps the residue of old gum. Then she returned to the table.

When she got back, Andrea and Mike were deep in conversation with each other, but Elinor didn't want to seem bothered by that and instead decided to talk to the British guy and his girlfriend. She turned her body toward them and tried valiantly to block out the insistent gurgling of the badinage behind her.

"So how do you know Mike?"

"We know Andrea actually," said Tomas. "I'm an intern at *Harper's*. Andrea was an intern there before she left to get a job at Memo Points Daily."

"How cool!" said Elinor with a sinking feeling. *Harper's* was just the thing that Mike would be impressed by, and that Elinor was also impressed by.

"It's great. I had to call up John Cheever's estate to fact-check something the other day."

"Wow. What do you do?" Elinor said to Vivian.

"I'm an editorial intern at *Harper's*," said Vivian. "But I'm leaving soon to go to *n+1*."

"Okay," said Elinor, miserably. She was feeling the alcohol. In this new light, Tomas seemed to have a simpatico demeanor.

"I had an interview today," said Elinor. "At a website."

"Which website?" said Tomas.

"Journalism.ly?" said Elinor.

"What is that even like? How *was* that?"

"I bet that must have been really funny," said Vivian. "What's Sean like?" She seemed embarrassed for Elinor. Then Elinor worried if what she'd said was embarrassing. This often happened to her when she drank. The next morning was a day of recriminations like Yom Kippur.

"Yeah, I don't know," said Elinor, hurriedly. "I didn't meet him. I don't know if I'd take it if I got it. I'm trying to freelance mostly."

"Did you read that article about the woman who decided not to work at all for a year? She just freelanced. But then she got really in debt," said Tomas.

"Yes," said Vivian. "Amazing."

"She thinks the world is both far too obsessed with working, yet at the same time, underemployed," said Tomas. "But it's interesting, maybe we really are transitioning into a full-freelancer economy? And what does that really mean?"

"Excuse me," said Elinor. "I have to get another beer."

. . .

"Hi," said Elinor.

"Okay, whoa," said Mike. He was trying to lift her down the stairs and into their apartment, but it was hard because Elinor had locked her knees.

"Did you have fun tonight?" said Elinor.

"Not as much fun as you," said Mike.

"I love you," said Elinor. "I like your haircut." Mike had gotten an interesting new haircut recently. The top of it was flopping awkwardly around his ears even though the sides of it were very short. Elinor actually hated his haircut, but now that she was drunk she was convinced she had to tell him she liked it because otherwise he would figure out that she hated it.

"Did Andrea give you your new haircut?" Elinor asked, and laughed. Somehow this joke had sounded funnier in her head.

"Did Andrea tell you how she cuts her own hair?" asked Mike.

"No," said Elinor.

"It looks great. I had no idea."

After Mike unlocked the door to their apartment, Elinor pushed it open. The apartment was so messy. All the dishes she owned were in the sink and there were only three. Mike set her down on the foam pad and went over to their kitchenette. He got Elinor a cloudy glass of water and brought it back to her.

"Drink this," he said.

Elinor nodded. She took the glass in two hands and she drank the water. It was probably a dirty glass. It had a thumbprint on it. A depression settled over her.

"Mike, I really want this job," said Elinor.

"E," said Mike.

"And I just don't think I'm going to get it," said Elinor. "I'm so worried. I felt like I didn't even say anything good during the interview."

"It's going to be fine," said Mike. He got up from the pad. Elinor watched him put on a black T-shirt that read "This Is What a Feminist Looks Like" and red, thin, plaid pajama pants. Then he lay down on the foam pad.

"I mean, maybe it wasn't that bad. I don't know." Elinor took off all of her clothes, quickly and with her back to Mike even though he wasn't looking at her. Then she crumpled next to him on the foam pad. She hugged his back. It was so bony, not much bigger than her own back. It might have been smaller.

"I remember," said Mike in a sleepy voice, "how worried I was during this whole interview process. And look, I got the job. And now I have these great friends. Weren't they so nice?"

"Yeah," said Elinor.

. . .

Weeks later, Elinor was sitting with Ramona and Fraunces in their Park Slope apartment. They were all in the living room, playing. Ramona had these blocklike Swedish dolls she was obsessed with, and she was lining up all of the dolls' shoes in a row. The shoes were tiny and unstable, and Ramona wanted them very close together in a very straight line. It was an impossible task. Every time one of the shoes fell over from some inadvertent knock, Ramona would get extremely mad, and put the shoe back with unnecessary vigor. Then the whole line of shoes would fall down. Then Ramona would cry and make Elinor put all the shoes in a line again.

Elinor had a splitting headache. Today, Mike had gone to his first day of work at Memo Points Daily. He'd left two and a half hours early that morning because he "wanted to get an early start."

"You didn't put the shoes in the right line," said Ramona.

"Yes, I did. Which one didn't I?"

"This one." Ramona pointed to a shoe that was slightly crooked.

"Okay," said Elinor. "But this is the last time I'm going to put these shoes in a line. They always fall over."

"Do it," said Ramona in a dead voice, moving aside so that

Elinor could have full access to the line of shoes, which were standing precariously, just waiting to be brutally knocked over.

Elinor was putting a green Mary Jane next to a red Mary Jane when her telephone rang. It was an unknown 212 number. Elinor's stomach seized up.

"Why is your phone ring the sound of a dog barking?" asked Ramona in an accusatory way.

"Woof woof," said Fraunces. He took his pacifier out of his mouth. He looked at Ramona in a prideful way.

"Fraunces, you have to stop barking because I have to answer the phone." She tried to make some obliquely quieting motions with her hands. Fraunces barked even louder.

"Ramona," said Elinor, watching her phone light up again with the ghostly visage of an unknown 212 number. "Can you play with him?"

Ramona gave a nod of acknowledgment and went over to Fraunces's Legos and stood above them in a detached way. Fraunces stopped barking, put his pacifier in his mouth, and showed Ramona a Lego. Elinor picked up the phone.

"Hi, Elinor," the phone said. Elinor recognized the voice on the other end as J.W. She barely breathed.

"I just wanted to congratulate you. You got the job at the Journalism.ly, congratulations."

"Oh my god! Thank you!" said Elinor. "That is so amazing. Wow, thank you so much."

"Yeah," said J.W. "Anyway, you start on Monday. Is that okay?"

"Of course," said Elinor. "Of course it's okay."

"Good," said J.W. "See you soon then. Welcome to the team."

"Goodbye!" said Elinor. A job! A job in journalism! Elinor looked at Ramona and Fraunces. Ramona was putting one Lego on top of another in a desultory fashion.

"Who was that?" asked Ramona. She looked at Elinor shrewdly.

"My new boss," said Elinor, with glee. "I'm getting a new job. Can I play Legos with you guys?"

"You still have to do my shoe line," said Ramona.

"Oh," said Elinor. "I forgot about that. Thank you, Ramona."

Ramona nodded. Fraunces was hitting two Legos together, as if they were tambourines. They were making a very loud noise. Elinor started to take Ramona's shoes and put them in the line. Ramona came over and watched her, like a factory manager in Soviet Russia. About two minutes later, Elinor knocked the entire line of shoes down accidentally with her elbow. Ramona cried piteously.

Chapter 4

Facebook: 1 post: "I have a really exciting announcement! Next week, I start work at Journalism.ly [hyperlinked]! I'm so lucky and grateful for this opportunity and I can't wait to start working at such an exciting place. From the time I was a little girl, I have dreamed of becoming a journalist, and now it is all coming true! #grateful #lucky #journalism #proud #goals." 123 likes, from almost everyone, even strangers.

Twitter: 21 tweets. A lot of Journalism.ly articles. Perhaps she is bragging as well, slightly? Sample: "Such a meaningful amazing essay. Wow." (Link to something called "What Reading Harry Potter Taught Me About the Middle East.")

Instagram: 2 pictures of Mike. One of the top of his head, crouching over his legal pads with his back to the camera. Caption: "Hard at work! I hate to pull him away, but I must! We're celebrating my new job! #proud #memopointsdaily #journalismly."

The second, a picture of Mike's eyes and forehead. He is wearing glasses. His hair is askew, as if he just woke up. The light is dim as if it is the morning, but it is in fact the afternoon and the light is dim because of the prison bars. Caption: "#bae."

. . .

That night, Elinor got home earlier than usual. Generally, Ramona and Fraunces's mother wanted her to stay for dinner, but tonight she and her husband were going out and taking the kids with them to visit their friends from Sweden at a Swedish restaurant, so they didn't need her to stay. It really couldn't have been more convenient. Elinor had texted Mike about the new job, and he had texted back "Congrats!!!!!!!!!!" but nothing much more than that. She hoped they could go out to dinner tonight or something and talk about it.

The apartment was dark when she entered it. The one light source in the room was Mike's laptop, which seemed to be open on a Word document (she had never caught him being distracted or looking at websites). She could hear Mike's voice. He was talking on the phone. Elinor put her bag down in the hall next to the door.

"No, Mom, I didn't," said Mike to the phone. "And I don't know what you're talking about." There was a pause. "I don't think she's like that. I think that's incredibly unfair." The pause was longer.

"Mike?" said Elinor. "Is that your mom?"

"One second," said Mike.

"Did you tell her I got the job at Journalism.ly?"

"Oh, Mom? Elinor just came in. Yes. So shut up. She wanted me to tell you she got the job at Journalism.ly. The one you set her up with? Yeah, yeah. Elinor, my mom says that's great."

"Can you hand me the phone? I just want to thank her myself?"

"Okay," said Mike. He handed Elinor his iPhone. She heard some scuffling on the other end, and a silence.

"Pam?" said Elinor. "I just wanted to say thank you so much about the job."

"I'm glad to hear it."

"I'm so excited. Thank you so much!"

"I'm very happy for you," said Mike's mother.

Elinor tried to think of something to say. She rubbed her forehead with the hairs of her forearm and the hairs stood up. "Well, uh, I should probably give you back to Mike?"

"No, no, it's okay. I've got to go anyway. But we'll see you at our Memorial Day party? I was just going over the lists for all my parties this year."

"Oh yes!" said Elinor. Mike's mother gave a Memorial Day party every year. Elinor was really excited about it. It seemed like a good networking opportunity, which was an important part of being a journalist, which she soon was going to be. Last year, a columnist for the Metro section of *The New York Times* came!

"Great, great," said Mike's mother. "Bye!"

"Bye!" said Elinor.

Elinor turned toward Mike and gave him his phone back. It was not the most satisfying conversation, perhaps, but that was how talking to adults was—full of pauses.

"Your mom is so nice," said Elinor. "It was so nice of her to help me. And like, look how it all turned out!"

"Yeah, you got the job," said Mike, who turned and looked

at his computer again. He even looked like he was going to start typing.

"How's your story?" asked Elinor.

"It's whatever," said Mike. "I'm not done, but I can't keep working on it tonight."

"Want to go out to get some dinner?"

"I already ate."

"You did? But I texted you I was leaving early."

"I didn't get a text. Maybe you thought you sent it, but you actually didn't."

"Check your phone," said Elinor.

Mike sighed. He took out his phone and scrolled through the messages with his thumb. "Oh, okay, I see it. I didn't see it because my mom called, I'm sorry."

"I guess I'll just get Seamless."

Mike didn't say anything.

Elinor went over to the minifridge and poured herself a glass of water from the Brita. The water was warm and tasted of iodine. The Brita had only recently been refilled. She felt a swell of self-pity.

"It's okay about tonight," said Elinor, in an injured voice, crouched near the refrigerator. "We can get dinner or something this weekend?"

"Actually, El, I think I might pitch that story to Kevin I was writing about the waste management plant in Queens, so I should probably go out there this weekend." Kevin was Mike's boss, who was one year older than Mike, and Mike seemed already to regard him as a surrogate father.

"So you're going to be gone all weekend?"

"No," said Mike, in an abrupt way. "I'm not."

"But, are we even going to celebrate the fact that I got a new job?"

"Elinor, come on! Give me a fucking break, okay? I just started a new job." Mike sighed. "I'm really happy for you. But I'm just working my ass off, and like, who knows what your job will be like?"

"Well, I think it's going to be an intense job. It's not going to be this lame thing. I think I'll probably have to work pretty hard."

"I don't think you'll have to work *that* hard, El. Which is good! But we'll see. I mean, congrats, hon. I'm proud of you."

Elinor was silent.

"Are you mad or something?"

"I'm not mad," said Elinor.

"I'm congratulating you. Okay?"

"Okay."

"I don't get it," Mike yelled. "I don't get what the fuck I did. You always take offense to every single fucking thing."

"I just think this job is going to be really hard, okay?" said Elinor. "I'm probably just stressed."

"God." Mike looked at what Elinor could now see was a blank Word document. "I feel like we're always fighting."

"We're not fighting," said Elinor. "I don't think we're always fighting."

"I just feel like you're always mad at me."

"I'm not," said Elinor. "I'm really not."

Elinor felt like crying. Why was she mad? What had he even said? She walked over to Mike's desk, and placed her hand next to his computer. "I'm sorry. I have just been so stressed for so long about this job thing and being unemployed and stuff. I've been waiting so long for a job."

"It's fine."

"We should do something fun this week," said Elinor brightly. "I'm serious. Do you want to go to Sheila's party? She's having some people over for drinks."

"In Murray Hill?" said Mike. He wrinkled his nose. "Ugh. I actually can't anyway. The office is having this networking thing, or I guess more of a drinks thing, from six to eight p.m. Especially because I just started I feel like I really have to go. It's really good networking."

"Oh, okay."

"Maybe we could meet up after?"

"Yeah, sure," said Elinor. She wasn't really surprised. Although Sheila had always liked Mike, Mike had never liked Sheila. Mike didn't like any of her friends. They never talked about anything he liked to talk about, he said. They just talked about boys. Sometimes Elinor became embarrassed for them if they talked at all while Mike was around, because that was true.

"I'm going to order Seamless," said Elinor. She took out her computer and sat down on the foam pad and proceeded to do what she said she was going to do.

. . .

On Monday, Elinor got to the Journalism.ly at 9:00 a.m., when J.W. had told her to arrive. The lights were off in the stairwell. When she finally climbed all the stairs, there was no one stationed at the reception desk in the lobby. The doors to the main office were locked. After a short interval of jangling the doorknob of the Journalism.ly to no avail, she sat on the chair near the reception desk. She tried to read current events on her phone. She was reading an article called "We Could Solve Congress by Employing This Swedish Technique" on Memo Points Daily when a man came up the stairs.

This man had long brown hair and was wearing tweed trousers and yellow suspenders, but in a way that seemed purposeful. Without saying anything to Elinor, he opened the door with several keys from a huge key ring. The Journalism.ly office had five different locks.

"Hi! I'm Elinor," said Elinor, while the man in the suspenders was unlocking the third lock, seemingly unaware of her presence. "I'm a new employee? Today's my first day."

"Oh," said the guy. He had a low, bored voice. He stared at her, neither friendly nor unfriendly. "Why're you here so early?"

"I was told to be here at nine a.m."

"Nobody gets here until eleven at least. I get here the earliest of everyone and that's literally to unlock the door. Most people work from home in the morning. Come in," he said. Elinor walked behind him into the office, abashed.

"I was gonna make some coffee if you want any," said the guy, rapidly turning on the lights all over the room with one switch, like in a gymnasium. He darted toward the kitchen.

"Sure."

Elinor wasn't sure if she should follow him so she just stayed in the main newsroom, looking at everything. The whole setup seemed roughly the same as what she remembered—but bereft of people, more fleeting and amateur. The tables seemed flimsier. The floor had black marks on it, like it had never been cleaned since some heavy machinery had been removed.

"So what do you do here?"

"What?" the guy yelled from the kitchen. Elinor walked closer to the kitchen entrance and hovered around it. Inside, the man was making coffee.

"So what's your job here?" asked Elinor in a quieter voice.

"I do the office shit. And I open the office," he said, scooping the coffee into the top of the coffeemaker with a rotund metal spoon.

"Do you like it?" asked Elinor.

"Yeah," said the guy. He fastened the lid on the top of the coffeemaker. "The coffee will be ready soon. I have to go open up Sean's office."

"Okay," said Elinor. Then the man walked out of the newsroom, and presumably into Sean's office. Elinor sat down at a table near the window.

For the next hour, Elinor sat at the table. Someone had penciled "WTF?" on the corner of the table in very small gray letters. The suspenders guy never came back. Occasionally, she helped herself to cups of coffee in the kitchen, to give herself something to do. There was something wrong with the coffee. It still had grounds floating in it.

At around 11:00 a.m. people started trickling into the office, all carrying laptop bags under their arms. Everyone who worked at the Journalism.ly was pretty young and seemed visibly depressed to be at work. On entering the newsroom, they immediately helped themselves to the coffee and sat at tables where Elinor wasn't sitting. Elinor didn't see anyone she knew or who had hired her. A part of her wondered if she should go around asking people what she was supposed to do, but a larger part of her thought that would be annoying and that it was appropriate to wait.

At 12:00 p.m., right when Elinor was wondering whether she should get lunch and what it would be, J.W. walked through the door. He was carrying a fake leather briefcase. He was wearing a light blue shirt open at the neck. Elinor stumbled up from her seat and lunged toward him.

"J.W.!" she said. J.W. looked at her as if she had roused him out of a trance. He blinked slowly.

"Hello?" he said.

"It's me, Elinor. It's my first day."

"Oh yeah, that's right," he said. "Do you have your computer?"

"No one told me to bring one?" said Elinor.

"Yeah, you have to bring your computer from home," said J.W., who started walking quickly across the room. Elinor followed him, not quite knowing where he was going. He stopped next to a table where five other people were sitting.

"Sit here," said J.W. "I'll get you a computer. But you can't keep it. It's our spare computer."

"Okay," said Elinor. She sat down at her new table, and J.W. walked away, presumably in search of a computer. All the people at her table were typing furiously. Elinor looked over the shoulder of the girl sitting next to her and realized she had four chat boxes open and they were all blinking maniacally.

After about ten minutes, J.W. came back. He was holding a bulky and obscurely dirty Apple computer, which he laid out in front of Elinor.

"Okay, here," said J.W.

"Thanks," said Elinor. "So, what should I do exactly—"

"I'll let you know in a minute," said J.W. "Right now, I've got a lot of stuff on my plate with partnerships."

"Okay! Just let me know," said Elinor. J.W. sighed and went into a conference room with glass walls. Elinor could see him in there. He was staring at his computer but not typing on it.

Elinor opened her computer and decided she would read everything on the Journalism.ly, industriously, until J.W. came back. For example, right now, the lead story was something called "The Real Problem I Have with Democracy," next to a picture of an empty Senate building on a cloudy day. If you clicked on the picture of the empty Senate building, you could read that article. Another headline was "Why the Republicans Are Wrong About Solar Power," next to a picture of the sun. If you clicked on the sun you could read a four-hundred-word piece about solar power that started with the sentence "There is a lot of stupidity about Solar Power out there, but Rep. Jim Thomson (R-CO) epitomizes exactly the kind of regressive thinking that no one can stand." Next to that was a list called "10 Cute Things That Make Adele Your Best Friend."

After Elinor finished reading all the Journalism.ly, she started Googling the company. Elinor found a recent article about Journalism.ly in Memo Points Daily almost immediately ("What Journalism.ly Needs to Do in the Online World [And What It's Not Doing]"). The thrust of the article was that Journalism.ly claimed to disrupt journalism, but that no one read it ever. "Sean Patterson's Journalism.ly made a lot of promises and didn't deliver. Instead of disrupting the space, it's an unmitigated flop."

Elinor felt a numbness that settled in her throat when she finished the article. Was it true? Was she working at a terrible place? Did Mike think thoughts like that? But Journalism.ly looked almost exactly like Memo Points Daily, which looked exactly like BuzzFeed, which looked exactly like something called TheBuster.com, which looked exactly like NewYorker.com. They all had a mix of opinion pieces, lists, and dutifully reported news, like a Facebook feed. How was there even a hierarchy of any kind? Maybe Journalism.ly had slightly more lists than most of the others—but was that so bad?

At some point, she stumbled on an article from 2012 called "Is This Man Hacking Journalism?" accompanied by a picture of Sean Patterson, the CEO of the Journalism.ly, holding a newspaper and ripping it in two and then standing on newspapers that were crumpled up on the floor. Sean had large eyes with protrudent bottom lids. He had curly, thinning hair that was flecked with gray. He was wearing a T-shirt and Converse sneakers. Under the picture it read: "Journalism is broken, we need a new model."

Elinor read the article and she learned some useful information. Sean's father knew a lot of journalists. (As a child, Sean had played catch with Bob Woodward.) At some point, Sean became a venture capitalist in Silicon Valley and then he realized that the old model for journalism doesn't work anymore.

"No disrespect to my dad or anything," Sean said in the article. "I just don't think telling people what to think works anymore. I think they make their minds up for themselves. That being said, great journalism never goes out of style— which is why we have some accomplished investigative reporters working alongside new-media innovators. That's the special mix that we're bringing. You can be smart and stupid at the same time." Elinor wondered if J.W. was an accomplished investigative reporter. He was the only old man here, so it was probably so. The thought filled her with the shamefaced conviction that she had not treated him with enough deference.

She decided to email that article to Mike with the subject line "Cool!"

It was now 1:00 p.m. J.W. was still sitting in the conference room and staring at his computer but not typing. Was there something she should be doing that she wasn't? Should she get up and talk to J.W. even though he said he was going to come back and talk to her? She could get lunch, but what if she was called to do something during lunch? There seemed nothing to do but introduce herself to her seatmate. Elinor tapped the girl next to her on the arm.

"Hey," Elinor said. The girl looked a little startled, but took off her headphones and placed them on her neck. The headphones were giant white conical spheres. The girl had pointy ears, messy hair, and makeup all over her eyes.

"Hi," said the girl, very quietly. "Sorry, I'm just on Adderall. I was zoning out. What's up?" The room was extremely quiet. No one else was speaking. There was only the tapping of keys, pittering in the background like a gentle drizzle.

"Hey, so, no worries, sorry to bother you." Elinor was embarrassed now at the loud and hollow sound of her voice. "But I'm new here. My name's Elinor."

"Hey," said the girl. She held out her hand. "Oh my god, I'm like, shaking a little. Do you see that? Look at my hand. I'm Nicole."

"When did you start working here?"

"Like, a couple of months ago."

"Cool! Do you like it?"

"It's stressful." Nicole got pinged on chat; it echoed faintly through her headphones. Her chat box changed from blue to red.

"Oh, fuck this bitch," said Nicole.

"What?" said Elinor.

"She's saying that my story 'Cats Explaining Feminism to Me' is like, too much like this story she's doing."

"What?"

"Ugh. What a bitch. It's so not."

"Wow," said Elinor.

"I know, right," said Nicole, who didn't look up from her screen. She was still typing into her chat box.

"I'm trying to figure out what to do today, actually."

"Has J.W. told you?"

"Not yet," said Elinor.

"That sucks," said Nicole. "Well, what's your name? Let me add you on Insta and stuff. Nice to meet you." Once she got all of Elinor's information (her full name, her Instagram, her Snapchat, her Yik Yak, her Ask.fm), she put her headphones back on.

Elinor went back to looking at her computer screen. She tried to find Sean Patterson on Facebook and realized that there were a lot of Sean Pattersons. At some point, during the progress of Elinor's reading, Peter walked to the front of the room, his hands clasped behind his neck. Elinor didn't notice Peter was standing there until he cleared his throat loudly.

"Attention, everyone. Please stop what you're doing. Sean is coming in. There's an all-hands meeting in two minutes. I think he's bringing cake." Peter smiled as if he had made a joke. No one looked up or laughed or acknowledged what he'd said. Then he walked quickly into the kitchen. Nicole made a face and took off her headphones.

"Oh god no." She must have been listening through the headphones. Were the headphones even playing music?

"Why no?" said Elinor.

"I hate these," said Nicole. "I actually really have a lot to do today and I had the shittiest night last night, like the fucking worst night of my fucking life."

Elinor heard some vague commotion behind her, so she turned around. J.W. had emerged, bleary-eyed, from his conference room, and was shaking hands with a man in a cashmere sweater and jeans. It was Sean Patterson.

Sean Patterson's hair was slightly grayer than it looked in the picture, and he was shorter, but more muscular. (He had large and not particularly attractive circular muscles that wrapped around his rib cage. You could see them through the sweater he was wearing.) He wore very dirty sneakers despite his old face. While talking to J.W. he kept patting him on the back. Eventually, he strode up to the front of the room, followed by a ghostly girl holding a cake box.

"Hello, everyone," said Sean, who settled himself next to an empty plastic folding table. The pale girl put the cake on the table. "How are you all doing?"

People mumbled in stilted assent. Sean had a high but commanding voice that articulated certain words very forcefully.

"I wanted to call this meeting because, well, I think it's important for all of us to be on the same page in terms of all the new initiatives we're bringing on here in the run-up to the election. This is a very, very exciting time at the Journalism.ly," said Sean. "It's a big time for change."

Sean smiled broadly, showing white, square, capped teeth.

"Look at this room. We have some of my favorite journalists in this room." Sean paused. Everyone tittered nervously, not knowing, perhaps, whether this was a joke. "Peter is one of my favorite journalists, Dwight is one of my favorite journalists, and Josh, of course Josh. Let's give Josh a round of applause for his new piece—'Despite the Carnival, the Party Decides.'"

Everyone clapped halfheartedly, and an adenoidal twenty-four-year-old with a bald spot took a bow. Elinor saw J.W. looking at the floor, his hands balled into fists.

"But in order for us to provide some of my favorite writers to the world, we need to concentrate on some revenue-growing activities. And that's why we really need to concentrate on something I talk a *lot* about—going viral and adding video! Because I really do think this business will be at some point profitable. I really do. I just think we need to really focus on trying to do that. But at the same time, never sacrificing the great journalism that has made Journalism.ly a guardian for the public sector! I don't want to make anyone nervous, I just want you guys to know what's important for the purposes of transparency. And we also have cake, guys, which is pretty sick."

Sean gestured to the cake, which was being cut up and laid out on the table by his ghost/assistant. Then he walked purposefully toward J.W. and started talking to him in a low and confidential voice. They eventually wandered toward the conference room, at which point most people in the newsroom wandered up to the front of the room and took cake slices, silently. Elinor got cake too. She helped herself to a large slice and sat back down at her table. Nicole ate her cake with her headphones on.

Elinor ate all of her cake, which was dry and tasted faintly of lemon even though it was ostensibly vanilla, and wondered about what to do. As J.W. seemed busy for the rest of the day (it was now kind of late), Elinor decided she should probably talk to Peter about what to do. He seemed to be in charge.

Peter was sitting at the table where the cake had been (now deserted of people; the cake had been moved to an unseen locale). He too was wearing headphones and typing. A narrow slice of cake lay untouched next to his computer. Some crumbs had dribbled onto the paper plate the cake was on, like he had dragged his fork across the cake, almost eaten it, and then decided against it.

"Peter," said Elinor.

"Uh, hi," said Peter, startled. He took his headphones off, and they clattered on top of his computer keyboard. He sighed like she was interrupting important business, even though Elinor could see all he was doing was chatting into various portals.

"I'm just wondering if you had any idea what I should be doing? This was my first day and no one has really said what exactly a special viral content editor is—"

"Well, what do you think you're supposed to be doing?" Peter leaned back in his chair.

"I don't know." Elinor said this more quickly than she meant to. "No one has told me anything. I've been here since nine a.m. and I haven't seen anything that would tell me what I would be doing."

"Well, this position takes a lot of initiative, Elinor. That's the first aspect of any job. Take initiative."

Elinor was torn between a sharp sense of injustice and a deeper fear that perhaps she had not been doing the right thing by continually Googling random topics. Guilt colored her future comments.

"Well, I didn't even know what I was doing for sure."

"You are replacing Elizabeth," Peter said, gazing at her in a fixed way. "What I want you to do for the next couple of days, I just want you to get a feel for the site. At the end of the week, I want you to come up with a viral thing that goes viral. Maybe like something bad that happened to you. Or a funny list. You can look up what Elizabeth did. And then just upload it to the site, I'll email you directions on how to do that. I'll try to look over it when I can, but don't feel the need to run everything by me, because this job is about initiative. I do more investigative journalism? I'm writing a piece about how millennials are the first generation to switch jobs a lot and how that's actually good for them—"

"Well, that's not really an investigative journalism piece," said Elinor. "That's more like an opinion piece."

"No, it's an investigation piece. I'm calling people, like this psychologist."

"But still, you have an opinion. The opinion is that it's good for them. That's an opinion piece."

"No. Not really. I think that's actually false objectivity," said Peter. "Anyway, have any questions on your job?"

"No," said Elinor, even though she did. She trudged back to her table.

She sat down next to Nicole again.

"So, do you know what your job is?" asked Nicole, without taking off her headphones.

"Kind of," said Elinor.

"That's so fucked," said Nicole.

Elinor stared at her computer screen. The enormity of her task paralyzed her.

Luckily, Elinor could see a bunch of people getting up and going home. It was about 6:00 p.m. Elinor waited for Peter to get up from his seat, which he did, at 7:30. Then she left out the same door.

Chapter 5

Social Media Blackout

(Unusual since 2010)

. . .

The worst day of Elinor's life hadn't seemed like it was going to be the worst day of her life when she woke up that morning. At first, it just seemed vaguely shitty: It was raining a little and only tiny shards of light were coming through the prison bars on the windows of the apartment. Mike was gone when she woke up, but she knew he had to get up early today because he wanted to work on his new story in his #knowyourtrash series. She had run out of coffee and she had only forty-six dollars for the rest of the month after she paid her student loan, so she couldn't buy any.

Another thing that Elinor had to do that day was finally come up with a piece of viral content. All week, she had been pottering around the office trying to think about what to write that would go viral, and her uselessness was starting to seem excessive. Every day, on the subway ride into work, she lambasted herself for her lack of ideas. But once at work, she looked at her emails and picked at a small scab on her knuckle between two long hairs. She had already looked up what Elizabeth had done, and it was only one piece ("Why I'm Glad to Be a Spinster in the 21st Century") and it didn't seem to be all that helpful. Everyone had seemed far busier than she was, clacking importantly on their keyboards, blinking obtrusively, laughing silently at the end of the day at the messages they'd missed on their phones.

What did people even like to read? It was so hard. Elinor liked to watch videos of animals, but there were a lot of animal videos on the site every day anyway and she was never fast enough to post them.

Unfortunately, when she got to work that day, the coffee was even worse than usual, completely grounds and two inches of cloudy water. She brought some back to her seat but couldn't drink it. And since, Elinor reasoned, it was impossible to work without quality coffee, she went to Dean & DeLuca, even though she didn't really have money for the extravagance.

At the counter, she asked for a drip coffee.

"We don't have that," said a woman in a chef's hat. "Is an Americano okay?"

"Sure," said Elinor.

She waited for her Americano at the coffee bar. It was relatively deserted, so she looked out the window at the people walking by. It had become forbiddingly cold all of a sudden, and the pedestrians seemed cowed. They were uniformly walking with their heads bent and their hands shoved violently in their pockets.

"Americano," the woman behind the counter said. Elinor took her cup off the coffee bar and the heat of the liquid burned through the cup and seared her hand. She had forgotten to get a sleeve. She took the cover off the coffee, blew on it, and took a sip. It was still scalding hot, which made her hand move involuntarily and spastically sideways.

"Shit!" said Elinor. The coffee cup was also too full of liquid. It spilled slightly, damaging the seam of the cup and burning her wrist.

"Ow, fuck!" But at the very same moment she was swearing loudly, she also got an idea. Everyone drinks coffee. What if she wrote a list of all the things that are just so coffee?

Elinor ran back to the office. She jumped up the stairs two at a time.

. . .

At 6:00 p.m., starving and too nervous to keep sitting, Elinor got up from her chair. She had just finished her list and put it up on the website. It was called "15 Things Only Coffee Lovers Know." She had tweeted, Facebooked, and Instagrammed it from Journalism.ly's account, which was what she was supposed to do. She was done for the day. But, as all the quotes about writing did say, it is a vulnerable business, and Elinor felt suddenly exposed. She hoped this piece went viral.

"Where are you going?" asked Nicole, who looked up at her curiously. Elinor never really ended the day with any type of finality. She usually waited until everyone else left and skulked out behind them, not even putting her coat on until she was far down the stairwell, in case she was asked, midexit, to come back inside.

"I'm going to my friend's party." Sheila was having a party tonight. Elinor didn't want to go. She just wanted to go back to her basement and watch old sitcom reruns and refresh her computer.

"Sounds fun. I'm going out for drinks and then maybe to like, this *n+1* guy's house. He's a nice guy, but all of the guys he hangs out with are kind of terrible. I don't know why I'm going. I hate books by men."

"Ugh. Yeah."

"Well bye," said Nicole with an air of dismissal. "Have fun at your party!"

"I will," said Elinor. She gathered up her stuff and headed to the subway, virtuously, even though it was a little bit dark outside like it was going to rain and any normal person with more than forty dollars to her name would take a cab. On the subway, she tried not to think about the fate of "15 Things Only Coffee Lovers Know" by zeroing in on the subway ads of Dr. Zizmor, a very sad-looking dermatologist who seemed to specialize in almost every medical ailment.

. . .

Sheila lived in a large seventies-era tubular apartment building with six other girls. Originally the apartment was a three-bedroom, but it had been subdivided with many ingenious-looking fake walls, some of which were simply fashioned out of very large bookcases. The apartment itself had a real kitchen with a stove and a dishwasher, and the lobby had a doorman and an elevator. Elinor was really jealous of it, even though Mike said that Murray Hill was so douchey he could never live there.

By the time Elinor got to Sheila's apartment, the party was fairly crowded, and to her chagrin, Elinor didn't recognize many of the people inside. Perhaps they were nurses Sheila worked with at the hospital. There was a series of different-size bottles laid out in a row on the kitchen island (replete with straw barstools! What an apartment!). The TV was on, playing an episode of *The Real Housewives of New York City*, but there was no sound coming out of it.

Elinor sat on one of the barstools and was in the process of making herself a vodka soda when she saw Sheila gliding toward her. She was holding a beer and wearing a red V-neck sweater. Her hair, which was brown, was remarkably straight and adhered to the sides of her head as if it had been slicked there with an oil. Usually her hair poofed out at the sides.

"OMG, hi," said Sheila. "I'm so glad you came."

"OMG, of course!" said Elinor. "Did you do something to your hair?"

"Yes! I got a Brazilian blowout!" said Sheila.

"It looks good," said Elinor, trying not to look at it. Sheila really did have terrible style. The longer Elinor was in New York, the more she realized it.

"I think it does look good! Once the oil gets out of it, or something. I don't know why it looks wet."

"It doesn't," said Elinor. "Not that wet. You can just wash it or something."

"Ralph isn't here yet," said Sheila, touching her hair, perhaps physically relating the two thoughts in her mind. "And I don't think he's going to come."

"Did you invite him?"

"I felt like I had to. Because we're friends. It would be mean if I didn't anyway, because we talk every day. But now I don't even think he's gonna fucking come at all. So I don't actually know why I invited him."

"I bet he'll come," said Elinor with a conviction she actually felt. She was sure Ralph would make some important appearance or nonappearance. He was always coming to things and not coming to things in a way that freighted his arrival (or nonarrival) with meaning—like the titular character of a play.

In the corner of the room, behind a large leather couch shaped like an L, one of Sheila's roommates was motioning to Sheila to help her put a handle of rum into a plastic bowl poised on a coffee table. Apparently they were making a punch.

"I have to help her," said Sheila.

Elinor checked her phone. "15 Things Only Coffee Lovers Know" was doing pretty well, she thought. It already had five hundred shares and three comments. One of them, from some-one named Mimi52, said, "Lol, I do this." Elinor smiled at her screen. Unfortunately, that pleasant reverie was ruined by Peter, who was somehow entering this party and was putting his coat on a chair piled with coats.

Elinor quickly found Sheila near the punch bowl talking to her roommate. It was an emergency, so Elinor grabbed her arm and said, "Can I talk to you for a minute?" in a fake friendly but purposely strained voice, so Sheila would know that she was actually upset.

"What?" said Sheila. "Is Ralph here?"

"No. But, did you invite Peter?"

"Yeah." Sheila pasted an oily lock next to her ear. "What's the big deal?"

"How do you even know him?"

"You always forget that I was a communications major too," said Sheila, huffily. "I know all the same people you know."

"But I don't even know Peter."

"We're Facebook friends so I just included him on the Facebook invite. I don't really know him either. I thought you said he was your boss." Now Sheila was mad, Elinor could tell.

"I mean, I do know him. It's so awkward though. He's always really awkward with me."

"That's weird," said Sheila, who seemed, suddenly, very bored by this story, but more probably was still mad, as Sheila was usually inflamed by mild, unspecific acts of rudeness. It was her greatest strength as a friend. "Well, you don't have to talk to him."

"I know that, I just, he's my boss sort of and I hope he doesn't think that I'm a total slacker or something because I'm at this party."

"Elinor, that's so dumb. *He's* at this party. I have to go to the bathroom. It'll be fine, okay?" Then she walked toward the bathroom—a large amber marble monolith with huge mirrors that Elinor was also jealous of.

In the ensuing pause, Elinor checked her phone again. "15 Things Only Coffee Lovers Know" had seven more comments.

When she looked up from her phone, Peter was standing near the punch bowl, a mere five feet away from her, blankly putting liquid into a Solo cup. It seemed as if he was going to try to affect a look of fake absorption in his task so that he wouldn't have to say hi to her. Elinor wasn't originally going to say hi to Peter, but she definitely wasn't going to stand for this particular treatment. Now she was going to be extremely outgoing.

"How's it going, Peter?" she said.

Peter looked up from the punch bowl shocked, like he was famous and someone had popped up from the inside of a trash can and asked for his autograph. "Uh, hi," he said.

"It's Elinor from work," said Elinor.

"Peter," said Peter, reaching out to shake her hand.

"I know you!" said Elinor.

"I know," said Peter. "Hi, how are you."

"Fine."

Peter blinked rapidly. "I saw you put something up before I left."

"Yeah, 'Fifteen Things Only Coffee Lovers Know.' I think it's really going off great."

"We'll see. Are you enjoying your first week at work?"

"It's stressful but good," said Elinor truthfully. Despite her doing absolutely nothing all day, it was actually the most stressed out she had ever been in her life. "And Mike's starting a new job too, so—"

"Mike who?"

"Mike Moriarty? My boyfriend?"

"Oh, him," said Peter. "He's your boyfriend?"

"How do you not know that Mike is my boyfriend?" Elinor felt a dull panic, which soon transfigured with a reassuring rush to anger. "Of course you know that."

"When you mentioned him in the interview I just thought

we had a mutual friend," said Peter, with a disturbing equanimity.

"I'm around him *all* the time though. It would be weird if we weren't dating."

"I've never seen you together."

"Yes, you have. I had dinner with you."

"I don't remember that. Sorry. It's not a big deal."

Sheila approached them then.

"What's up?" Sheila was holding a beer and seemed mollified. Her hair was slicked back into a braid. She must have done that in the bathroom. "Is Mike coming?"

"Mike, my boyfriend?" said Elinor. "He has to go to this thing at work."

"Really? That's cool." Sheila had taken out her phone and was texting on it. Elinor couldn't see who she was texting. "Hey, Peter, good to see you."

"Uh, thanks," said Peter. "I'm going to get a drink. Does anyone want anything?"

"No," said Sheila. Peter shuffled away toward the wineglasses and started pouring himself a fresh glass of wine, even though Elinor was pretty sure his Solo cup wasn't actually empty.

"He's nice," said Sheila.

"Yeah," said Elinor. "I think he's such a dick."

"He seems nice to me." Sheila texted. Elinor looked at her phone too.

"Okay, Ralph is FaceTiming me. I don't even know why, but I should probably take this. Ralph? Ralph? Hi." Sheila wandered dreamily away, looking at a miniature distortion of Ralph's face, and Elinor was left alone again.

Elinor decided to get a drink even though she didn't want

one. Luckily Peter was not even near the table where the wine was anymore. More people had arrived at the party and she couldn't see him in the crowd. Maybe he had left. She unscrewed the plastic cap on the wine box and poured a little, with shaking hands, into a red Solo cup. The wine tasted like potpourri. Elinor took a large swig and, glass in hand, walked toward the TV. She didn't feel like talking to anyone.

She sat down on the L-shaped couch. The leather upholstery was baggy, and Elinor picked up about an inch of it and rubbed it between her index finger and her thumb. On television, she watched as some blond woman went into a blindingly white mansion and talked to another blond person with sunglasses on.

After ten minutes or so, Elinor became engrossed in the show. She was thus completely unaware of the fact that Peter was also watching *The Real Housewives* on the other side of the L couch, his arms embracing a cushion balanced on his stomach. When she noticed him, she stopped rubbing the upholstery with her thumb.

"So do you like this show?" said Elinor.

"I've never seen it before."

"Do you want to know what it's about?"

"I don't really watch stuff like this," said Peter.

"Okay," said Elinor.

They both watched the show for ten more minutes.

Eventually, she said, "Okay, I gotta get another drink."

"Bye," said Peter, not looking at her.

Elinor didn't actually get another drink. Instead, she picked up her bag and grabbed her coat, and said goodbye to Sheila, who was very upset. Ralph had FaceTimed her to say he wasn't going to come to the party. Sheila had agreed to this on the phone, and then had sent him several angry texts after he hung up. This meant that he was probably going to come to the party, but very late after everyone left, and Sheila had cried profusely.

Elinor went back to her apartment. This time, however, she took a cab. She didn't want to, and it used up a lot of her forty dollars, but it was dark out.

. . .

When Elinor got back to the fake wooden door of her apartment, which blocked no sounds, she was startled because she heard muffled voices coming from inside the apartment. Was Mike having a party he didn't invite her to? She could hear a song—some warbling man singing over an electronic beep. A girl was in there. Elinor heard her voice.

Elinor didn't dream at all at night, but she had very complex daydreams involving shattering scenes of emotional distress. So she had thought a lot about what she would do if she went home and found that Mike was cheating on her, even though Mike would never do that. Would she be shocked or would she stand there stolidly and yell, "I knew it." Would Mike yell, "I can explain!" Would he cry? Would Elinor scream?

Elinor turned the key in the lock and got the door open. Inside the apartment, there was Mike, Andrea, and some other guy Elinor had never seen before, who was wearing a whisper-thin, gigantic T-shirt that was clearly quite expensive. His hair was white blond. He was fiddling with the computer. Mike and Andrea were sitting on the foam pad, talking to each other.

"Hello!" said Elinor, brightly.

Mike looked up from Andrea. He made a face at Elinor. It was a very brief face. A flicker of the eyelid. A stiffening of the jaw, maybe. Had something in her voice showed that she was upset that Andrea was there? Did she seem annoyed? She wasn't even upset really, when she thought about it. When she thought about it more, she was just surprised. That's all she was.

"Hey!" said Mike. He waved to Elinor from the foam pad, but he did not get up. "How was your party?"

"Peter was there," said Elinor.

"Peter?" said Andrea. "Your friend Peter? Oh my god, I love him."

"Isn't he the best?" said Mike. "Elinor always hated him."

"I never hated him," said Elinor, "I just didn't really know him before and now I work with him." She crouched down to the minifridge, took the Brita out from the back chasm, and started pouring some water into a glass. Why would Andrea know anything about Peter? Did she meet him at some point when Elinor wasn't there? Elinor took a sip of water.

"You think Peter's a dick?" said Andrea, affecting a sort of lawyerly attitude and crossing her ankles on the foam pad (hard to do).

"Oh, Elinor definitely thinks Peter is a dick," said Mike. "Like, a hundred percent."

"I never said that," said Elinor.

"That place must be stressful, though. Like, I bet he's just stressed having to crank stuff out like that. I like that we can take time to write," said Andrea. "We're not as dependent on deadlines."

"How was your party?" said Elinor.

"Ours?" Andrea pointed at herself. "It wasn't really a party. It was more of a work drinks."

"There wasn't enough drugs," said the kid with the big T-shirt on. He had a hat on too. It had graffiti on it.

"E, do you know Matt?" said Mike, gesturing to the kid.

"Uh, no, I don't. Hey," said Elinor. The kid just nodded at her.

"I see him everywhere," said Mike. "He was just at the bar where our drinks thing was. He goes to everything."

"Do you guys work together?" said Elinor, trying to smile at Matt, who was absorbed in the laptop of music.

"No," said Mike. "But he knows Jeremy."

"Did you talk to Jeremy?" asked Andrea to Mike confidentially.

"Who's Jeremy?" said Elinor.

"He's our editor in chief," said Andrea. "Such a cool guy."

"No," said Mike. "He was talking to David the whole time."

"That sucks," said Andrea. "I know you wanted to talk to him about that story."

"What story?" said Elinor.

"Look, guys," said Matt. "I'm going to bounce. I got things to do and places to go." Matt chortled when he said this, as if he was so visibly original that such a cliché was necessarily ironic. Everyone else laughed too, like they agreed.

"Hey, man, sorry," said Mike. He stood up and gave Matt a strange elaborate handshake Elinor had never seen him do before.

"Cool," said Matt. "Well, bye." He snowshoed summarily out the door.

Unlike most people, Andrea did not take this as a cue to vacate the premises. On the contrary, she seemed to almost settle in, sit lower and deeper on the foam pad, as Mike returned to his perch beside her. Mike might have later said that Elinor seemed to not like Andrea for no real reason, but there was a real reason. The real reason Elinor hated Andrea was because she was always being rude and not picking up on obvious social cues.

Elinor stood by the kitchen counter and checked her phone. Her story had ten thousand views. That was actually pretty good for a piece of content on Journalism.ly.

"You know, I actually wrote a piece today, and I think it's doing kind of well!" said Elinor, apropos of very little. "It has like, ten thousand unique views?"

"You guys track how many views your piece gets?" said Andrea. "Darren is really against that. I mean, we know generally how things do, but we don't know the actual number of views something gets. He thinks it completely ruins the writing process."

"Yeah," said Mike. "I actually think only one guy in like, the entire organization knows how anything actually does."

"That guy Chris?" said Andrea.

"Yeah, Chris. I think he's the only one to see the actual numbers."

"LOL, Chris is so weird," said Andrea.

"I know," said Mike.

Elinor walked over and sat on the foam pad on the other side of Mike. This way, even though they were all on the foam pad, she could also rest her head against the wall (the foam pad lay right against a prominent crook in the wall—none of the walls was straight in the whole apartment; there was always some unnatural divot) because she was tired. When she looked back on this moment, because later in her life she thought about this moment a lot, she never wavered in her conviction that her tiredness at that point could not be helped. She really was extremely tired. She just wanted to let her body stretch out on the floor like she was dead. But she didn't even do that! She actually just rested her eyes a little bit with her head against the wall. Was that so awful? Was that really so bad?

"Okay, well, I think I'm going to go," said Andrea. "Elinor is like, basically asleep. I feel bad."

"Oh, you don't have to go," said Mike.

"No, I should," said Andrea. "It's late and I have to get up early tomorrow."

"No," said Mike. "I'll go out for more beers."

"Nah, we got to get up early tomorrow," said Andrea. "I'll see you at the office?"

"No fun," said Mike. "Boo!"

"Bye, Andrea," said Elinor. She got up from the foam pad and shook Andrea's hand. She yawned loudly because she was tired. That was the only reason.

Andrea got up and ambled toward the door. Mike walked her down the hallway. They were saying something to each other that Elinor could not quite make out, and then Mike loudly said, "See you tomorrow," and the door slammed. Elinor started putting on her pajama pants.

"You're putting on your pajama pants?" said Mike, when he came back from the doorway.

"I'm super tired." Elinor yawned again.

"What was up with you tonight?" said Mike.

Elinor put her college sweatshirt on. Mike rested his hand against the small table of the kitchen. His fingers drummed against the Maxwell House. This was making Elinor even more tired.

"Nothing," said Elinor.

"Oh," said Mike. "I hope Andrea wasn't mad you just sort of lay on the ground while she was here. She had to go home. I know she felt awkward, which I'm sure was your intention."

"She didn't have to go home because of that."

"Yes she did," said Mike. "It was a cue to go home."

"Uh, okay!" said Elinor. "I'm sorry for being tired?"

"You're always sorry."

"What?" said Elinor, dazed. She propped herself up against the wall and drew her blanket around her legs.

"Like, you just did a really shitty thing. You were like, falling asleep while we had guests here. It was so rude."

"It wasn't rude," said Elinor, blinking. "I'm so tired. I just had the shittiest day. That party was so—"

"You always have a shitty day," said Mike, sarcastically. "Everything's always a mess."

Elinor was awake now.

"I don't think that's true. At all. I mean, maybe it wasn't a shitty day, maybe it was more stressful."

"It absolutely is," said Mike. "You were just so fucking rude for no reason."

"I'm not rude. Having random girls here without asking me, now that's rude."

"Elinor, what? What?" said Mike, yelling now. "I didn't have a random girl here, Elinor. Andrea is my friend. She's my friend, okay?"

"Well, you didn't come to Sheila's party with me, but you bring Andrea here?"

"Oh my god, Elinor," said Mike. He was angry. "You are always so unbelievably ridiculous. This is outrageous. You're rude to Andrea, and now you're taking it out on me?"

"I'm sorry," said Elinor, quietly. "I know she's your friend. It's just that I was tired."

"It's the worst," said Mike. "She's just a friend. She's just a fucking *friend*."

"Okay," said Elinor, blankly. This was suddenly so serious and hysterical. But how did it even get this way? Now Mike was sighing loudly.

"I feel like we're always fighting," he said.

"No we aren't."

"Yes we are."

"Couples fight."

"Not like this," said Mike. "I've just felt like the past year has been such a fucking mess."

"No it hasn't," said Elinor. She heard her voice get higher as she spoke. "What are you talking about? No it hasn't!"

"Like, our apartment sucks," said Mike. "We don't have a bed. We live in this wack place on the Upper East Side. I wanted to live in Brooklyn like a normal person, and you picked this weird-ass apartment, with a superlong hallway."

"I didn't know you really wanted to live in Brooklyn," said Elinor. "I picked the apartment when you were living at your mom's and I couldn't find anything—"

"Everybody lives in Brooklyn!" said Mike. "Everyone!"

"Okay, no!" said Elinor. "Sheila lives in Murray Hill and I picked this place because they—"

"Anyway. We've been fighting a lot and there's just been a lot of tension. And I feel like you want me to do things with you all the time. But I have my own life, okay? I can't always be making you feel okay! I have to have my own life."

"I know that," said Elinor. She got up off the foam pad and walked over to Mike. His eyes had a watery film over them. She tentatively grabbed his hand and rubbed her thumb along his palm, but he didn't even hold her hand. He just stared over her shoulder, like he saw something on the other side of the room. Elinor felt a pinprick of panic. Although she and Mike often fought (as you, dear reader, have seen), he had never made such apocalyptic allusions before.

"Elinor, why are we doing this?"

"Doing what?"

"Fighting all the time," said Mike.

"Couples fight."

"We need to take a break. We can't keep doing this to each other."

"What?" said Elinor. She started backward. "What are we doing to each other? What?"

"I just think we need to take a break. This isn't working."

At first Elinor felt nothing when he said that. She felt like she was watching the movie of her life and someone had stopped it in the middle and panned out and it wasn't in Elinor's head or point of view anymore. Elinor felt sad for this Elinor she was watching, in an odd, fuzzy way. Then she felt a dull ache in her stomach like she was going to vomit.

"I just, I came home," said Mike. His eyes were full of tears. Plop plop plop went the tears, Elinor thought nonsensically. She almost laughed. "And I had had this great day at work. This really amazing day. And I just wanted to be here with my *friends,* okay? And you just come in here and go to sleep? You make it so uncomfortable that Andrea has to leave. My god. And I should be excited to share my day with my girlfriend, you know? But I just wasn't. I wasn't excited to tell you anything about it. And that's not right."

"I think I'm going to vomit," said Elinor.

"I think things have been wrong for a while," said Mike. He sniffled, but he wasn't going to cry, it seemed. He was just going to get choked up.

"How have they been wrong for a while?" said Elinor. Her voice was hoarse. She couldn't help it. "I never noticed they were wrong. I mean, we fought sometimes, but all couples do. Everyone fights. I mean, we *live* together."

"I don't know, E," said Mike. Although his eyes had filled with tears, now he seemed calm in a way that was almost more frightening, like the previous hysteria had been some kind of theater, and now he was getting to the real meat of the thing, the crux of his emotional being, and there was no time or inclination for the sluicing of sentiment that had come before. "I have a new job. And maybe I am too consumed with my career at the moment to be in a relationship, and that's unfair to you too."

Elinor stared at him dumbly.

"I love you, Elinor," said Mike. He took her hand. His eyes turned beseeching, which because of its suddenness, made Elinor feel as if it was also a self-conscious choice, like he had seen someone act this out before. What was happening? She needed to think! "I do. I just wonder if we need to be apart right now. I mean, who knows what can happen between us? We might just need some breathing room."

"Please," said Elinor in a small voice. Was this really going to happen? Was Mike really going to leave her? She was going to have to move because she had fallen asleep. It was all over.

Without warning, her mind flashed to the time when she had looked up her and Mike's astrological signs when they first started dating. In the beginning of their relationship she was constantly looking up signs that she and Mike were meant to be. She Googled numerology, she took quizzes in the backs of magazines. The best part of it all was that she was a Taurus and he was a Virgo. They were actually the most compatible signs of the zodiac. Everyone else was with less compatible people.

"Oh god," said Elinor. "Please don't go. I mean, I'll do whatever you want. I'll change in any way you want. I won't get as jealous. I'll change. But I wasn't even mad anyway, I'm just tired."

"I'm definitely not sure this is the end of us, but I think we do need a time-out. I'll pay my share of the rent for this month, so at least you can stay here and figure it out."

Elinor started to cry. The sounds of her crying made her even sadder. This was the worst thing that had ever happened to her in her life.

Chapter 6

Facebook: 1 post. Caption: "Sometimes, you just need to see some good news when you've been sobbing all day." Link: "The Cutest Thing You've Ever Seen: A Monkey Takes a Bear Under Its Wing." In the still image, previewing the video, a monkey is wrapped around a bear's neck. The monkey looks like it's strangling the bear, but maybe the bear actually likes it. One comment, from Elinor's aunt: "That is so cute! Hope you aren't feeling too down. What's wrong?" No answer from Elinor.

Twitter: 23 tweets. Sample: "Take this quiz to realize whether you are a psychotic murderer! The results may surprise you #Murderquiz." (Link to article.)

Instagram: No pictures, but 2 quotes—a bad sign. The first? "What doesn't kill you inspires you later." The quote is in white script on a black background. The second: "Happiness is a decision you make every day. People who don't want you to be happy aren't helping that decision. Haters to the Left." That is in pink script on a gray background. Lots of likes. Some comments of the "You go, girl," variety.

Snapchat: A video of a crowded bar, Botanica! The camera scans the tops of heads. "Wait a Minute" by the Pussycat Dolls is playing faintly in the background.

. . .

just can't believe it though," said Elinor. "I can't. I can't believe it!"

"Did you think you were going to marry him?" said Sheila in a drawling voice. Elinor was sitting in Sheila's apartment on Sheila's L-shaped couch. It was three in the morning, but Sheila was happy. Ralph was there. Ralph was sitting on the other side of the L-shaped couch, playing a video game on a gigantic TV that stretched in front of them like *The Last Supper*.

Mike had offered to leave the apartment and sleep somewhere else for the night. Elinor had pleaded with him not to do that. Instead she left the apartment. She didn't take any clothes and then took a cab to Sheila's. She had taken two cabs that day! She had only twenty-five dollars left. Looking back, she didn't quite know why she was so dead set on Mike staying put in their apartment. Maybe she didn't want to think of him calling Andrea, or sleeping on a couch at a friend's and actually saying, "Elinor and I broke up," to that friend. Sheila was surprised to see her and probably pissed at first, considering Ralph had made his entrance at 2:00 a.m., after the party.

"I don't know if I thought that," said Elinor. "I mean, I don't know. I guess so? I never really thought about it. But yeah. I mean, we were living together. Maybe I thought we were going to end up together. I mean, of course I thought about it, but

I wasn't always thinking about it. I wasn't obsessed with it. I mean, he just said we're taking a break. I'm not even sure we're broken up. It could have just been a really bad fight."

"Yeah, I know," said Sheila. They didn't speak for a while. The only sounds in the room were from Ralph's PlayStation. Something violent was happening on-screen. Elinor watched it like a zombie. Ralph was driving a car and then occasionally he would get out of the car and kill a woman who looked a bit like a prostitute. Then he would get back into the car and drive away.

"Do you think I wasn't cool enough?" asked Elinor. That was one of the things Elinor had always been worried about with Mike. Elinor felt like she was cool sort of, but not really. She didn't really look that cool. She was a journalist, which was a cool job. But she felt like Mike, in his ideal world, would like a girlfriend with a cooler job—maybe someone who didn't work at the Journalism.ly, but who did cut her own hair. A hipster girlfriend. She just knew he would want that.

"I don't know, maybe?" said Sheila.

"What do you mean, maybe?" said Elinor sharply. "You think he did?"

"I don't know, Elinor. You always said that. I'm just going off what you said. Hipsters are stupid."

"God, that would just be the worst," said Elinor, whose eyes started to brim with tears. "I really hope that's not it."

"Oh, it's not," said Sheila. "I was just agreeing with you. I don't really think that. Mike's just going through a rough time right now. I'm sure he'll come to his senses." She patted Elinor on the back. "Ralph, can you finish this game? You've been using the TV for like, an hour. When are you going to be done?"

"I'll be done in ten minutes," said Ralph.

"You said that thirty minutes ago!"

"Your fucking friend is here."

"Ralph!" said Elinor.

"Shut up, Ralph," said Sheila, but she didn't really seem annoyed. Ralph played his video game in silence.

"I'm going to make popcorn," Sheila announced to the room, but mostly to Ralph. Ralph acted as if he had not heard her.

Elinor drearily followed Sheila into the kitchen area. Sheila put a bag of popcorn into the microwave and slammed the door. Elinor was still wrapped in a fleece blanket with the logo of their college embossed on the front. She pulled the blanket around her head like a cape with a hood and sat on a straw barstool positioned against the island.

"How are you feeling now?" asked Sheila. The popcorn popped helpfully in the microwave.

"Still shitty," said Elinor.

"At least you like your job?"

"I don't. I really don't like my job."

"You are going crazy," said Sheila. "You have to stop this. You can't just freak out and ruin your life."

"I know that, Sheila," said Elinor. "It's just been like, six hours or something since I got horrifically dumped by my live-in boyfriend. Jesus fucking Christ."

"Okay, whatever, sorry," said Sheila. She took the popcorn out of the microwave and placed it, delicately, in front of Elinor. Elinor tore open the bag even though it was really hot and burned her fingertips. She ate a huge handful of popcorn and scalded her throat.

"Fuck," said Sheila. "I'm so tired. I can't keep waiting for him to give up the television. Do you mind if I go to bed?"

"Not at all," said Elinor. "Can I stay here tonight?"

"Of course," said Sheila. "You can sleep on the couch. Is that okay?"

"Yeah, that's fine," said Elinor. She walked back to the couch. She curled up in a ball and laid the college blanket over herself. Then she watched Ralph play video games until she fell asleep.

. . .

After a dreamless sleep that almost felt like a coma, Elinor woke up on Sheila's couch the next day. She was half awake for five minutes when she realized that Mike was gone and that she was sleeping on a couch and not a foam pad. If not for that, however, it seemed like it almost didn't happen.

She woke up to the sounds of Sheila making coffee.

"Do you want a cup of coffee?" Sheila stage-whispered at her from across the apartment. Her fingers were laced around a blue clay mug. She was already wearing her scrubs. One of her roommates, a tall girl with very puffy hair, was standing near her, and looking suspiciously at Elinor.

"It's okay," said Elinor, feeling, again, sort of separated from her body. "I have to get to work."

"Okay," said Sheila. "Ugh, I have so much work today."

"Really?" said Elinor.

"Yeah, I'm working a double. And I'm so tired from last night. Not that you shouldn't have come over. It's just late for me to go to bed and my whole day is kind of shot."

"I'm sorry," said Elinor.

"It's fine. Are you still really upset?"

"Yeah," said Elinor. She felt a pain behind her eyes and in her nose, like she was going to cry. She blinked.

"You know," said Sheila, putting her mug down on the island. "I didn't want to say so last night, but I think it's still totally possible to get Mike back."

"Really?" said Elinor. "Why?"

"I think you should just go to him and be like, 'Listen, I'm sorry I fell asleep while your guest was there. That was rude of me.' I feel like that's all you have to do."

"Do you think so?" said Elinor.

"Yes, definitely," said Sheila.

"I mean, do you think it was really rude of me to fall asleep while Andrea was there?"

"I don't think it was rude necessarily." Sheila took a sip of her coffee. "He just probably felt like it was rude. All you have to do is apologize, I think. I mean, he likes you so much, Elinor. I know him, and I feel like he's a really sensitive guy. I just don't think you guys are broken up, you know?"

"So you think I should text him?"

"Absolutely," said Sheila. "But wait until the end of the day. I think the morning will seem too desperate."

"Okay," said Elinor hopefully. Maybe, despite the thrill of finality she'd felt last night, she and Mike weren't actually at cataclysmic odds. This would just be a really terrible fight they looked back on and laughed about. Later, she would say to Sheila, "I actually thought I was never going to see him again," but it would be over drinks, after she and Mike had already gotten back together.

"Okay," said Sheila. "I got to go. I'm already late and Ralph is still sleeping, ugh. Don't feel too terrible. This will all work out."

"Okay," said Elinor. "I'll walk out with you. Hold on for like, one second."

Elinor carefully folded the blanket she'd slept on and put it on the armrest of the leather couch. Then she went into the bathroom and put on the clothes she'd had on the night before, a knit dress, wool tights, and a pair of boots that had a square toe and came up to the middle of her shins. She looked in the mirror. Her hair was greasy. Her makeup had pooled in dim smudges beneath her eyes, and her skin seemed to be falling off in little, ruddy patches. Maybe she would buy new underwear at Victoria's Secret with the twenty-five dollars she had left to her name.

She walked out of the building with Sheila. The wind cut through her coat as if it didn't exist.

"Am I leaving you here?" said Sheila. "I just walk down First Ave."

"Yeah," said Elinor. "I'm going to take the N train to work."

"Okay," said Sheila. "Bye! Feel better."

"Bye," said Elinor, who walked in the other direction. She was fully intending to take the subway, but then she realized it was five or six blocks away. She hadn't noticed yesterday, but that was really a long walk. After a couple of minutes of walking in the direction of the subway, she found a cab, its number half illuminated, and took it. The ride cost sixteen dollars. She put it on her credit card.

. . .

Elinor got to work with some underwear she'd purchased at the local Gapbody stuffed into her handbag (two dollars on sale). She had cried only once during the cab ride and once in Gapbody.

As Elinor sat down, Nicole waved to her, palm open.

"Hi," said Elinor.

Nicole took off her headphones. She was wearing a sweater knit with a thick blue yarn and long black jeans that bagged at the knees.

"How was your party?" said Nicole.

"It was kind of weird," said Elinor, swallowing. She almost blurted everything out about Mike, but thought against it. What if it was like Sheila said, and it wasn't really that big of a deal? Then it would be stupid to say, "Mike and I broke up," when that didn't actually happen.

"Oh, too bad," said Nicole.

Elinor sighed and took her computer out of her bag. Work and its particular stresses poked through the haze of her misery. She waited for her computer to start.

"You must be happy this morning though."

"Why?" said Elinor in a dazed way.

"Because your coffee slide show did really well! Didn't you check?"

"Uh, no." Elinor rubbed her eyes.

"Yeah, it's like, a really big win for you! It got like, two hundred thousand page views or something last night."

"Really?" said Elinor, almost mustering up some interest. She turned her computer on and looked at the coffee story. It had actually done extremely well. There were twenty-eight comments! Someone with a blank face icon on Facebook had said, "I don't drink coffee that much. Sometimes I do. I don't like the bitter taste."

"Wow, it's up to three hundred thousand views now," said Elinor. "That's pretty good, right?"

"That's great," said Nicole, staring at her computer.

Feeling burnished by this slightly better news, Elinor decided to text Mike. Even though it was midmorning, Elinor theoretically thought that if you felt something, you should be able to text it.

Hey I miss you. Last night was weird. Can we talk today?

While Elinor was agonizing about whether to explicitly say sorry or to merely imply it, Peter stopped beside her. Elinor smashed her phone onto the table facedown.

"I saw your thing on coffee," he said.

"Yeah! I was happy because it actually did really well. Did you see that? Twenty-eight comments."

"Yes. I did." Peter looked at his foot, and Elinor waited for him to finish looking at it. Then he said, "Maybe you can pitch me your ideas two or three times a week."

"I have to run my ideas by you now? Why? Do you hate my ideas?"

"No," said Peter. "I'm just trying to have us be organized and work on a schedule."

"Well, okay?" said Elinor. "Are you my boss?"

"Not exactly. I just think my expertise in these matters could really help you. I'm really familiar with the tone here—"

"What does that mean? Do you think I screwed up the tone?"

"No," said Peter. "You need to listen to what I'm saying. Think of me more as a mentor."

"A mentor? But you're the same age as me."

"But I have more institutional memory here, like a mentor."

"You've been here four months longer than me!"

"You know, a lot of women are never mentored by anyone, especially men. It's really sad. That's all I'm trying to do here. I'm trying to help." Peter's face twisted into some kind of sad expression, and Elinor felt guilty.

"Okay," said Elinor. "I guess I'll run things by you now. Thanks."

"I'm really busy this week because Sean wants me to think about how we're going to incorporate tweetstorms into our coverage—did you see my tweetstorm about the debate?—but keep me in the loop and I'll try to get back to you when I can."

Elinor nodded at Peter, and he walked back to his desk. Elinor felt a new, sharper guilt on top of the enveloping guilt she was already feeling. Why did she have to snap at Peter? Still, at the same time, she was just having a shitty fucking day. Shouldn't she be allowed to have a shitty fucking day? For once?

She put her phone in her bag on the floor next to her leg so she wouldn't have to keep staring at it, but she put it on vibrate so if Mike did text her she would know and her phone would vibrate into her leg.

About two hours later, after many false alarms, her phone actually did vibrate into her leg. It was Mike.

Hey, I'm staying with friends for the time being. I got to go by
the apartment to pick up the rest of my stuff so why don't we
talk then? See you tonight?

    Elinor walked quickly toward the bathroom—a single room
with a toilet, a urinal, and no mirror. She locked the door
behind her and sat on the floor near the paper towel dispenser.
She closed her eyes and laid her head back on the wall.

. . .

When she finally got home, Elinor realized that Mike had not
been exaggerating about moving his stuff out of the apartment. Everything of his was gone. His legal pads, the "This
Is What a Feminist Looks Like" T-shirt. His drawers were just
wood.

    She wondered if she should have ever moved in with him at
all. At the time it had seemed only natural. She couldn't have
afforded the rent by herself and she knew Mike the best of anyone in New York besides Sheila, and Sheila was living with five
other nurses. Plus, she and Mike practically lived together in
college and they lived really close to each other in Chicago for
two years after college, so it didn't even seem like that big of a
deal. During senior year, they shared a twin bed.

    Mike said he was going to be at the apartment "tonight,"
but Elinor didn't know what time that meant and didn't want
to text him to find out because perhaps that could be perceived
as "putting pressure on things." She tried to distract herself. She
watched an episode of *Frasier* on her computer. She cleaned all
the dishes in the sink and saw that Mike and Andrea had been
drinking beers the night before—one of the glasses in the sink

had beer scum clinging to it. She squirted a mass of soap into the cup and tried to wash it out.

At 10:57, Mike arrived at the apartment. It was obviously raining out (it was hard to tell from the interior of their apartment what the weather was), as there was rain clinging to his collar and in his hair. Everything looked different about him somehow, even though the last time she saw him was yesterday.

"Hey," said Mike. "I just came back to get some of my stuff."

Elinor got up quickly from the foam pad and stood in the corner.

"You don't need to help me," said Mike. "It's okay. I barely have anything."

"Okay," said Elinor. She sat back down on the foam pad.

"I'm just coming back to get a couple of books," said Mike. He went over to an IKEA shelf they had installed right near the window and starting taking all of their books and putting them into a small canvas tote bag.

"Yeah," said Elinor. "I saw that you took most of your clothes."

"I was here earlier today," said Mike brusquely.

"Oh, okay," said Elinor. He must have moved all of his stuff out when he woke up. Did he take a day off? "Where are you staying?"

"I'm with Tomas for a couple of days. And then I think I'll head to my parents' for the rest of the month."

"Tomas? That guy from the bar?"

"Yeah. He's an intern at *Harper's*? Such a funny guy."

"I didn't realize you guys were such good friends," said Elinor. And she hadn't! When had they gotten so close to each other?

"Well, we are," said Mike. He had finished with the books

and opened the refrigerator and started taking items out of it, like the Gatorade. He was the only one who actually drank the Gatorade. "He lives in Crown Heights right near the Nostrand stop."

"So, I don't know. Is that what you're saying? That it's over?" Elinor started crying then. She couldn't help it. But Mike just looked at her, squatting down in front of the refrigerator, with the Gatorade in his hand.

"E," said Mike. "Listen, I really really need to concentrate on my work right now."

Elinor started sobbing harder.

"I do!" said Mike. He put the Gatorade on the floor. "I want us to take some time apart. We may end up back together. But I just need some time to think."

"You do?" Elinor wiped the tears off her face with a heavy hand.

"Of course I do!" said Mike, sitting next to her on the foam pad.

"But I don't understand," said Elinor.

"Listen," said Mike. "We talked this through last night. I'm really really busy with work and I know that you care about your job too. And we have so many of these really long-standing problems, which I've really identified. But I still want to be friends."

"I thought we were on a break," said Elinor.

"I thought about it more," he said, annoyed. "And I just think it's too hard."

"What?" said Elinor. "But last night you said we were on a break."

"I know I said that."

"Fuck you, Mike!" Elinor was hysterical. "Is everything you say totally meaningless? What should I do about the apartment?"

"Do *not* attack me," said Mike. "This is hard for me too and you need to understand that. As for the apartment I don't know, we went month to month on it. Why don't you just move out whenever. I don't think you can swing it for that long by yourself. Can you?"

"No," said Elinor. She gulped. "I just—" Moving was such an enervating ordeal. She had so much stuff and it was always multiplying. Just the other day, she'd opened a desk drawer that was filled with crumpled paper, old tights, and long hairs. How could she pack that?

Elinor's eyes started filling up with tears again.

"Hey, hey," said Mike. He put his arm around her. "Come here, what's the matter? What's happened?"

"I don't know, I don't know," said Elinor.

"Hey listen," said Mike. "We are going to be friends. I know we are. We just need to give this time."

"What about the Memorial Day party?"

"We'll figure it out. That's not for a while."

"Okay," said Elinor, and she turned to Mike and wetly kissed him. She stuck her tongue in his mouth and felt around for Mike's tongue. His tongue was limp. She shut her eyes so tightly that she could feel her eyelids on the bottoms of her eyes. Mike moved away from her.

"Elinor," he said, dry eyed, a little mad maybe.

"Don't go. I still need to talk."

"I have to, Elinor. I'm meeting Tomas." He had gotten up from the foam pad. Elinor still sat there.

"So you'll let me know in a couple of weeks? When you want to talk?"

"Yeah, definitely. I'll be back and we'll talk again, okay?" said Mike. He had gotten up and retrieved his bag of books and his bottle of Gatorade. He walked toward the door. Elinor followed him. She almost grabbed on to his shirt to keep him from leaving.

"Okay," said Elinor. She was crying now. She should have just felt sad, but her primary emotion was embarrassed. She was so ugly and fat, she couldn't even have sex with him as he was leaving, like any woman in any story ever before. "I love you, you know?"

"I know," said Mike. "I love you too! Have fun, okay?"

What did having fun mean? thought Elinor. "Okay," she said.

Mike shut the door behind him.

. . .

At work, Elinor could barely concentrate. Her mouth was always dry, and her thoughts looped in concentric circles. (Why did I fall asleep? But I had to fall asleep, I was tired. Can't a woman fall asleep? But why did I do it at that exact moment? What kind of person does that? But can't a woman fall asleep?) Occasionally, Elinor would forget what she was supposed to be thinking about. She would concentrate on an air-conditioning unit stuck moldering in a window across the way. She would wonder whether she would look good in a flannel shirt. But as quickly as this blankness came, a deeper nausea, a pattering heartbeat, a numb finger would remind her that she actually had things to think about, and she would go back to her thoughts about falling asleep.

She took a sip of her coffee and felt several grounds come into contact with her teeth. She felt like she was going to cry.

"Hey," she said to Nicole. Nicole was looking at some glossy cooking blog. It had a large bowl of dry lentils photographed in perfect lighting.

"What?" said Nicole.

"I don't know," said Elinor. "I just wrote a quiz called 'How to Tell Whether You Are a Psychotic Murderer or Not.' And it's doing well. But now I'm worried. How can this many people be murderers? Eleven percent of the U.S. population?"

"That seems high."

"Peter did sign off on it, but I wonder if he will think it's too inaccurate. He told me he's really worried about accuracy. Do you have to run all your posts by Peter?"

"No," said Nicole.

"Even when you first got here?"

"Never. He just told me not to get in trouble, write three posts a day, and not libel any of Sean Patterson's friends."

"Why do I have to? He's the same age as me!" said Elinor, her voice cracking. "How can a mentor be the same age as you?"

"What's wrong?" said Nicole.

"Oh god, I don't know," said Elinor. "I'm on a break with my boyfriend? I think?"

"Oh." Nicole's face crumpled into a sympathetic grimace. "Are you okay? I hate men. I mean, some are fine. I actually love a lot of them. Like, Josh is really nice. The politics guy?"

"I don't know," said Elinor. "I don't even know if we are on a break. Like, I think we are. I don't know. We got in a huge fight about nothing. Like, literally nothing. Like, I fell asleep a little early. And he got really pissed? And then all of a sudden he was like, 'I just need to concentrate on my job for now.'"

"Oh god," murmured Nicole. "That's so shitty. I bet you are feeling all the feels, ya know?" She kind of laughed.

"It *is* shitty," said Elinor.

"Well," said Nicole. "One time I went on a break, with the boyfriend I had before Rob? Mike?"

"Mike's name is Mike," said Elinor, sadly.

"What?" said Nicole.

"My boyfriend's name is Mike," said Elinor. "The one I'm on a break with."

"Oh," said Nicole. "Anyway, I went on a break with my boyfriend at the time, Mike. I loved him so much but I just couldn't with him. He had a very degraded relationship with his own sense of himself. He was really privileged in all these ways but he couldn't see that? He was like, *so* fucked up, but I was like, really attracted to that at the time."

"Yeah?" said Elinor.

"Yeah," said Nicole. "He was cheating on me?"

"Wow. That's terrible."

"Yeah," said Nicole. "I think he was cheating on me because his dad was a nightmare and he really had trouble dealing with it."

"That's horrible."

"We're still in touch. Like sometimes he texts me and that's fine. I'm happy to have him as a friend. But yeah."

"Ugh," said Elinor.

"I try to stay friends with all of my exes. I think it's very important. I mean, if they were important to you, why wouldn't they be important to you forever? But I really didn't know who I was at all then. I was so fucked up about my body."

"I feel like Mike and I will be friends at some point," said Elinor.

"You should write about it."

"Write about it?" said Elinor.

"Yeah, you should write an essay about it. To deal with it. I mean, he sounds like a real shit show to just freak out like that. I write essays all the time about what I'm going through. We can't just silence women's voices."

"For sure," said Elinor. "I've always said that."

"We're all single laydez now, you know? I should have T-shirts made. That would be so funny and like, pathetic."

"Yeah," said Elinor. "Wow."

It was at precisely this moment that Peter approached her table. She could see for the first time the tattoo on the inside of his wrist. What was it of? It was immediately obscured by a shirtsleeve, so Elinor never got to find out.

"Hey, Elinor," said Peter. "I've got to talk to you."

"What's up?" Was he going to fact-check her psychotic murderer quiz?

"Can we find a place to talk?" Peter craned his neck, looking about the room. He looked into the conference room, but J.W. was sitting there, playing a game of solitaire on his computer. "Let's go into the kitchen and get some coffee."

"Okay," said Elinor. She followed Peter to the kitchen. There was no one there. "What's up?"

"Okay. So Sean was really pleased by your coffee thing."

"Really?" said Elinor. She blushed.

"Yeah, it did very well on the site, even though it wasn't very topical, which was surprising to me."

"That's great."

"Yeah, it's interesting. Sean's been really interested in this idea of automating the success patterns—that's what he calls them—of some of our most viral posts. For example, a couple of months back Nicole did something called 'Animals That Look Like Feminist Icons,' and that did well, so now she's doing a bunch of different slide shows that are like 'Pieces of Cheese That Look Like Gloria Steinem,' and those have done really great. Do you get what I'm saying?"

"Yes," said Elinor.

"The trick to viral content is to mimic very closely what you did before and tweak it. That's why I just don't get this psychotic murderer quiz, when you could have done something like 'Fifteen Things Only Tea Lovers Know,' which would have repeated your success pattern."

"When I emailed you about whether I should do the psychotic murderer quiz, you said you were too busy to be emailed about my story ideas because Sean needed you to focus on 'Big Ideas About Music.ly,' which I took to mean that you were okay with me writing that?"

Peter's Adam's apple looked especially sharp and ridged. He said nothing.

"The quiz to see whether you are a psychotic murderer is doing really well!" Elinor continued, hotly. "It's doing even better than the coffee one, actually. Everyone wants to know if they are a psychotic murderer and I ask tons of psychological questions like 'Have you ever killed your pet?' So it's not just this crap thing."

"Okay, that's not the point of this discussion. The point is to come up with an automated system to make things go viral so we don't have to think about it as hard. Sean wants us to be faster and more agile."

"Okay," said Elinor. "I'll try and repeat my success pattern."

"Good."

"Can I ask you a question?" asked Elinor. "Why do you only look over my stuff?"

"I look over everyone's stuff. That's my job as managing editor. If I give you slightly more attention, it's only because I'm trying to mentor you because you are just starting out here, but I can stop if you want to."

"No, it's okay, I guess," said Elinor. She left the kitchen then, and headed back to her table.

. . .

Two weeks later, Elinor was sitting in her apartment alone, eating Top Ramen and looking at her bank account online. She had a worrisomely small amount of money. She needed to stop taking cabs all the time. Her rent was also now an exorbitant portion of her net worth. She really couldn't afford this apartment alone. If only Mike would come back and save her from moving.

Elinor decided to look at the room shares on Craigslist, just to see. She clicked on the first ad she saw. It was a little bit high for her price range but not horribly so. She read as follows:

Our apartment is super great and we all really love it. It has a great location (Williamsburg right off the Marcy Sto)p. We have a huge kitchen, a gigantic living room, and lots of light. We love people that are chill but very neat, and we all work a ton of the time and are never in the apartment, so if you do want to hang out in the apartment this place is not for you. Your room does not have a closet or a window, but the former tenant put a bar up with clothes hangers on it and that worked really well.

Elinor clicked through the pictures. There were many images of the living room, which was very large and did have windows, and the windowless and jagged triangle that was going to be her room. It didn't look that bad, but the problem was, what if she wanted to be in the apartment? She clicked on the next one.

Hey, we're a bunch of cool, very laid-back dudes that have an awesome apartment in Prospect Heights. We love to hang out in the apartment, chill, play video games, smoke, and play guitar late at night. Basically whatever. We're looking for any other roommate, girl or guy, who wants to chill with us in our apartment. Your room doesn't have a window or a closet, but a guy brought in this huge box thing/California Closet and he's willing to leave it if you pay him $150 bucks. Honestly, it works pretty well. Write us an email that's in the form of an epic poem.

Elinor quickly x-ed out of her browser. This whole evening was very stressful.

. . .

"And then he was like, 'We're on a break,' and so honestly, I don't really know what's happening," said Elinor. Her voice wavered at the end of this sentence.

"Dick," said Michelle. Michelle was their other friend, who was visiting from Chicago. She was staying on Sheila's couch. She was very tall and had a forehead like a plate. Her hair was curled into giant barrels that hovered in permanent suspended animation above her shoulders.

"He's not a dick," said Elinor. "I just think he wants to figure some stuff out."

"No one's saying he's a dick," said Sheila. She swirled a tiny red straw around in her Diet Coke and rum. "But he's not being the greatest right now."

They were at Botanica. Secretly, Elinor had been arranging all of her drinks dates at Botanica (or at least the ones with Sheila) since she and Mike broke up. She wasn't hoping to run into him, she said to herself. But if she did run into him, she would be functionally having drinks with Sheila and Michelle. It wouldn't look like she had spent days inside, hair matted to the side of her face, trying to understand from Mike's Instagram what he had been doing with his time.

"Have you heard from him?" said Sheila.

"Yes," said Elinor. "I mean, not since he moved out, but when he moved out, he like, told me and stuff."

"Mike's always been a dick," said Michelle.

"No he's not," said Elinor.

"Yes he is. Remember what an ass he was about living together?"

"Well, he just didn't know if he wanted to do that."

"He really left you out to dry." Michelle sipped her drink. "You couldn't live with Sheila because he was still 'deciding.' You had all those screaming fights. Then you were going to live alone, and he moved in with you because he didn't want to live with his parents anymore." Michelle never really had a boyfriend but she acted like she knew everything. She had been like this in college. She was always telling everyone to dump their boyfriends. "Plus he's so controlling."

"Controlling?" said Elinor. "How?"

"Well, he's always telling you how you have to react to stuff. The way he gets mad at you and cries? It's just because he's trying to control what you say to him all the time, so that you never say anything he doesn't like."

"I really don't get that," said Elinor. "I feel like that's really not him at all."

"Maybe you should go online?" said Sheila.

"Online, as in online date?" said Elinor.

"Yes," said Sheila. "A lot of people do it. I would do it if I didn't have this thing with Ralph."

"I mean, sure, I guess. Isn't it so weird though? Everyone I know hates it."

"No way! Everyone is online. I even think it's like, an empowering thing to do."

"Mike and I haven't really talked about dating anybody else. So I don't really know if like—"

"You still like Mike, right?" said Sheila, suddenly animated by her new idea. "Well, nothing is going to make him want you back more than you actually dating other people, okay? It will drive him nuts. Remember when I did that to Ralph in college? He flipped the fuck out."

"I don't know," said Elinor. "Mike isn't like Ralph at all. We have a completely different relationship than you guys do."

Sheila looked hurt.

"All men are the same," said Michelle, adjusting a barrel curl with her finger. It was at that point that Elinor, who was sitting on the chair that faced the door, saw Andrea come into the bar with Mike right behind her. She involuntarily ducked.

"Oh god, oh god," said Elinor. "Mike is here."

"What?" said Sheila, whipping her head around.

"Don't do that. Don't do that, okay? He'll see you. Just stare at me. Do you think he heard what we were saying?"

"I can't stare at you," said Sheila. "You're under the table."

"Elinor, the bar is super crowded. There's no way he heard anything. Who's that woman he's with?" said Michelle.

"That's Andrea," said Elinor. "They're friends."

"Ew," said Michelle.

"What are they doing?" said Elinor. "What's happening?"

"You can look, you know," said Michelle. "You're going to draw more attention to yourself like, ducking under the table."

"Okay," said Elinor. She slowly peeked over the table. Mike was at the bar, ordering beers, wearing a gray T-shirt that clung to his small yet protrudent chest. She could see his physical flaws—his too-small shoulders, his oblong head, the nostrils that weren't actually symmetrical at all—but somehow, he looked more attractive than ever. His hair was even more closely cropped on the sides. Andrea stood right behind him. Mike turned around and gave one of the beers to Andrea. Elinor turned toward Sheila, so that no one at the bar who happened to glance over would see her face.

"Okay, what are they doing now?" she said.

"Nothing that much," said Sheila. "She said something and Mike just laughed."

"Does he seem into her?" said Elinor.

"I think it just looks friendly," said Sheila.

"She's really not hot," said Michelle. Elinor somehow felt like she was going to cry when Michelle said that, even though it was a very comforting thought.

"Do you want to go?" said Sheila. She was already gathering her coat, so it was clear the answer should be yes, although weirdly Elinor wanted to keep watching them, or not watching them, but that was probably inappropriate.

"Okay," said Elinor slowly. She got up, gathered her coat, and put her canvas bag over her shoulder. The bag was heavy. It had her laptop in it.

"I just have to go to the bathroom," said Michelle. "I'll meet you guys outside."

"Okay," said Elinor, who was already standing up. She wished she was wearing a better outfit. This might have been the worst time in history to be wearing a turtleneck dress made out of Fair Isle sweater.

Even though she had been arranging her drinks here, hoping to run into Mike, she was not prepared for this brittle triumphalist meeting. In her ideal world, Mike would have been alone at Botanica, looking consumptive, drinking miserably, and their mutual, theatrical sadness would have formed an instant bond. Her lack of concealer and Fair Isle sweater would be appropriate for something like that. However, now that she saw Mike out with Andrea, she realized the error of her ways. She didn't want Mike to see her looking like this. Could she just slip out without anyone noticing? Mike and Andrea were positioned right near the door. Still, the bar was crowded enough that it might not even be an issue. If Mike saw her on the way out, she could avert her eyes and pretend she didn't see him.

Elinor started walking out the door with Sheila. She held her coat near her face in a way that she hoped looked normal but also blocked her from view.

She was walking right in front of Mike when Sheila blew up this (to be fair, completely uncommunicated) plan.

"Hey, Mike!" said Sheila.

Sheila waved to Mike and walked over and gave him a hug. Elinor paused midstep.

"Hey, Sheila," Mike said. He waved at Elinor, anemically. Elinor, unable to speak at all, waved back.

"We were just leaving," said Elinor, after a strangled pause.

"Okay," said Mike.

"Anyway, nice to see the both of you," said Sheila. Elinor walked quickly out the door and Sheila followed her.

"Sheila," whispered Elinor the minute they got outside. "Why did you say hi to Mike?"

"Well, how could I not say hi to him? It's weird if I didn't. I've known him for years. It's better than ignoring him. That actually makes you look way more weird if you ignore him."

"But," said Elinor, still whispering even though they were well clear of the bar, "I just wanted to get out of there."

"I think it was good," said Sheila. "It made you seem much chiller, as opposed to like, freaking out. I actually think I really helped."

"What just happened?" said Michelle, who had come out and joined them on the street.

"Nothing," said Sheila. "It was fine."

. . .

After they left the bar, Sheila, Michelle, and Elinor walked in the general direction of Sheila's apartment. No one really talked about seeing Mike or anything, even though it was the only significant event of the entire evening. Sheila prattled about this girl at work who was being a bitch about shifts, and Michelle talked about draining an abscess in an emergency room that had a lot of pus in it, even though everyone thought it was just a pimple at first. At one point, Elinor said, "Do you think Mike thought I looked insane?" and Sheila said, "We only saw him for like, a second," like she clearly did not want to talk about it. It was infuriating.

Eventually, Elinor made her excuses and started walking toward this French fries place she liked. It sold Belgian fries the width of a thimble. She got a large French fry and a milk shake. After that, she got a cab back to her apartment. Whatever! She couldn't eat fries on the subway. On the cab ride home she just stared out the window, thinking about nothing.

Once inside her room, however, Elinor got madder and madder. Maybe Mike really was a dick, like everyone was saying. People can fall asleep at any time! It's not that big of a deal. She took a beer out of the fridge and slammed the tiny fridge's door. Mike was such a piece of shit. Her friends were such pieces of shit. What the fuck was Mike doing with Andrea? He didn't even say hi to her or anything, and they were trying to be friends. He had never so much as written a text saying

"How are you?" since they ended their relationship. What the fuck was the matter with him? It was so rude! It was so impolite! What kind of person would do that? Elinor wasn't totally conscious of it, but she was still extremely drunk, even though she had had French fries and a milk shake.

She decided that she couldn't take this whole thing lying down. She was a strong woman. She was going to write Mike an email—telling him he could go fuck himself.

Hi

    So, I guess you don't want to be friends anymore or something. I saw you tonight and you were so rude to me. You didn't even say hi and like what? We were together for YEARS mike. The least you could do is be friendly and say hi. What the fuck is the matter with you. You are such a coward and your inability to say hi was really ridiculous. Don't be such a coward to not write me back either, that would just be the crowning fucking achievement of this whole fucking thing.

Elinor pressed send. Then she immediately started watching an old episode of *Law & Order.* After that, she went to sleep.

. . .

The next morning, a sunny but frigid Saturday, Elinor lay numbly on the foam pad, sometimes feeling a pulse of anxiety so violent she would roll onto her stomach and kick her feet. Her computer lay beside her, open. Mike had not responded to her email. Thinking about how Mike didn't say hi still filled her with anger, but in the light of day, she didn't know if her email had been wise. Occasionally, while flipping on her stomach, she thought it was. Other times, while lying on her back looking at Craigslist listings, she wasn't so sure. Maybe she had expressed herself too violently.

Apparently, last night she had also started a Tinder account. She didn't totally remember that. It was open on her phone when she woke up. Her bio line just said, "Trying to stay positive and get ahead in this crazy world :)." Was that wise either? She hadn't uploaded any pictures yet. Luckily she had decided to save that for a more sober time.

She chose two pictures. One of her and Sheila in which Sheila was laughing and Elinor was smirking with her mouth closed and therefore looked good comparatively, and one that Mike took of her when she was getting ready to go to a party. It happened to be Mike's favorite picture of her. She hoped he saw it and felt bad about it.

. . .

Two hours later, and racked with guilt, Elinor, wet from her shower, decided to text Mike an apology. Water plopped on her screen as she typed.

> I'm so sorry, I was so drunk last night when I emailed you. I didn't know what I was saying. I wasn't even mad lol. Can we meet up today please??

Mike never responded.

Chapter 7

Facebook: 1 post: "Ugh, sorry to rant here, but don't you hate it when you are literally cut in line again and again? Today, at a Starbucks, I was cut in line 3 times. Listen everybody, I get it. We're all in a hurry. But that doesn't mean that manners completely go out the window. Let's all have a little bit more kindness and compassion for each other, ok? Ok, Facebook rant over. Sorry. But jeez!"

Twitter: 22 tweets, mostly consisting of one surprisingly bitter Twitter fight between Elinor and a random Twitter critic of "10 Reasons Why Moving Sucks." A sample: "@dylan_84: If you think moving doesn't suck then I actually feel bad for you! You are probably privileged enough to have movers. #stopmoveshaming."

Instagram: 2 pictures. The first is of Michelle, Sheila, and Elinor, sometime during the week Michelle stayed with Sheila. They are out at a bar. Elinor especially has glassy eyes and a countenance of mournful forced merriment. Her mouth is in a pursed line. Caption: "Love my girls. #girlsnightout #lovethesegirls #sisters."

The second picture is mostly of Elinor's hand. She is in a light-filled café and there is a book and a coffee on a table in front of her. Her hand is on top of the book. It has been recently manicured. Caption: "Great Sunday! Reading at my fave coffee shop. #Whoneedsbrunch."

Snapchat: A selfie of Elinor drinking a smoothie. She is wearing a headband. Although she's slightly flushed, it is a very good picture, and one that she sends around indiscriminately. Mike doesn't open it.

. . .

J.W. was sitting in his conference room, looking at his computer, blankly, when Sean knocked on his glass wall, making a hollow little sound. J.W. slammed the computer shut and made an ostensibly welcoming motion to Sean, even though Sean had already walked into the conference room and was positioning himself heavily on a spare chair that J.W. had arranged artfully kitty-corner. He put one foot over the other knee and wobbled the gigantic multicolored tongue of his sneaker back and forth.

"Hey, man," said Sean.

"Hey, yourself," said J.W., immediately regretting it.

Sean set his foot on the floor.

"Anyway. Looks like traffic has been a little better."

"Oh yeah?" said J.W. He was still thinking about "Hey, yourself."

"We got a lot of views from that psychotic murderer quiz even though we couldn't sell ads on it. We might really be okay if we actually produce an engaged community." Sean said this with an air of hopeful wonderment. He lifted his heel out of the back of his sneaker. "Peter has been helping to mentor the girl who wrote that piece, he told me."

"That's great," said J.W., looking at the back of Peter's head through the glass wall. Peter was mentoring someone? Why? Wasn't he the same age as the girl he was mentoring? If anyone should be mentoring, it should be J.W.

"How are partnerships going?"

"Very well. Extremely well," said J.W. They were not going very well, but J.W. had recently completed his one corporate email for the day, so he did have a talking point. "I just emailed Vans sneakers."

"Sick," said Sean. "Maybe Elinor could do 'The Fifteen Things Only People Obsessed with Vans Sneakers Know.' I fucking love Vans sneakers."

"Great idea," said J.W.

"I love making things systematic," said Sean. "That's why I'm such a good investor. Because once you have a process you can just repeat it again and again and again and again. And that's what I want to install at Journalism.ly. A process that runs itself! When I was invested in that Tinder plug-in I was talking about? That's a classic example." And Sean proceeded to talk on and on and on about how he automated workflow at this plug-in for Tinder that allowed you to list your favorite lunch places in your Tinder profile. This was a story Sean liked to tell frequently.

. . .

After Mike didn't answer her email, a heavy weariness would often befall Elinor at work. She would drink a lot of coffee to combat it. As she carried her cup back to her seat, she would become preoccupied with the idea that she was going to drop it—the cup was always slightly too hot. She would picture the cup exploding into pieces, the coffee seeping into the floor and splashing onto open computers. She would even start to smell the peculiar, saccharine scent of coffee that had bled into wood and dried there. Then she would put the cup down.

At night she would try to sleep, but every time she would close her eyes, it would feel like someone had electrified her, and she would be filled with a morbid ether of nerves. How had she become so unattractive to Mike, so banal, so obliquely and consistently hideous? At some point during fucking her, had Mike looked at the immutable second roll on her stomach and felt disgust? He had never seemed as into sex as she had imagined men being. Was that because of her? Would he like it more with someone else? Did she pick at her skin in front of him, or only in the bathroom? She couldn't remember anymore. Maybe she remembered one time when she did pick at her skin in front of him. Did she smell bad? What did she smell like? Did she use too much tongue when she kissed? Was she boring?

It was the day after a particularly unspeakable night. Elinor was in her apartment, painting her nails a garish shade of electric blue that would occasionally drip into the protrusion of skin next to her nail. She was rubbing the side of her left index finger with a paper towel soaked in acetone when she realized she had a push notification from Facebook. Someone had invited her to an event.

To Elinor's shock, the Facebook invite was from Mike's mother. She had invited Elinor to an event called "The Memorial Day Party." Her Memorial Day party! Elinor was still invited. So Mike wasn't actually mad at her for her mean email. That was obviously what that meant—right?

She told Nicole about it the next day.

"So this is weird."

"What?"

"So I got a Facebook invite from Mike's mom to this party she's having on Memorial Day. Which is like, supernice of her. I was invited before, but like, now I'm still invited. But I'm just not sure I want to go now, even though I sort of feel like I have to go, because I'm really grateful to his family for everything they've done for me."

"I don't think you need to go," said Nicole. "Also that is a crazy early invite."

"It's two months early. That's not crazy. I don't know," said Elinor. "I said I would go. And like, what if I decide not to go, isn't that rude? Like, isn't that rude to his mom?"

"But I feel like," said Nicole. "And I could be wrong because I do not know this woman at all, okay? But I feel like that's kind of this thing that she'd understand, because you and her son broke up, what? Like, a couple of weeks ago."

"Fifteen weeks ago," said Elinor. "Yeah."

"I feel like she would just get that you weren't going to her party because of that."

"I don't know," said Elinor, skeptically. Because despite entreaties to the public for their counsel, almost immediately after getting the invitation to the Memorial Day party, Elinor had decided to attend it. She wanted to go to this party for a variety of reasons—the most conscious being that propriety seemed to demand it. Therefore it was dispiriting that so many of her friends were so unsupportive of the endeavor. She had thought they would have echoed her resolve and added something flattering to it ("Maybe his mother is inviting you because Mike has told her he misses you and he's afraid to email you back," for example). However, when she texted Sheila and Michelle, they both seemed to imply it was a bad idea for her to go to the party. Michelle actually said, straight out, she thought it was a bad idea, which was really kind of offensive. It was like they didn't even get that you could be friends with an ex, which was super-unevolved and closed-minded of them—but Michelle had always been like that.

At that very moment, J.W. approached her table. Elinor hadn't spoken to him since her first day. He looked older now.

"Hey, Elinor," said J.W. "Can I talk to you in the hall?"

"Good, um, sure," said Elinor. She had no idea why J.W. wanted to talk to her. Something bad was probably going to happen. The moving slide show had done slightly worse than the quiz about being a psychotic murderer. Could you be fired over something like that?

When they got out to the hall, J.W. smiled at her. He had a terrible yellow smile, like a shark beached on a sandbar.

"Elinor! I just wanted to tell you, you are really writing some interesting pieces. Which is good."

"Oh wow," said Elinor. "Thanks so much!"

"But, you know, you don't want to forget the rules of great journalism. Facts first. Tell the story. These are the types of things I know because I have been in the business for so long, and that is why I say—look at me as your mentor. You can ask me any question you want, and you should come to me if you have any questions. Don't go to Peter."

"Uh, okay. That's great. I mean, did I do the facts wrong? I know there are not that many people that are psychotic murderers. I would actually love more guidance. Should I write more about like, the election? I don't really want to go to Peter anyway so—"

"Peter's a good kid," said J.W., hurriedly, as if Elinor was on the precipice of saying something very offensive. "But please come to me if you have any questions. Do you know what you are going to write this week?"

"Um, I don't know yet. I've been brainstorming."

"Okay," said J.W. "Because I was thinking maybe 'The Fifteen Things Only People Obsessed with Vans Sneakers Know.' It's basically a takeoff on what you did before, but engaging more with branded content, but, of course, not actually being branded content."

"I'm not sure how well that will do."

"Well, I'm your mentor, so just do it," said J.W. He patted Elinor on the back and went inside. Elinor went back to her desk and started Googling Vans sneakers.

. . .

"And so that's really the tour of the place," said a girl with drooping eyes and a chin that blended seamlessly into her neck. She was going to be one of Elinor's future roommates if Elinor decided to take this apartment. She was holding a large chocolate Lab between her legs. The Lab had barked continually during Elinor's visit. It jumped up and down. It rolled on the floor. It begged for food. It scratched on some furniture like a cat.

"She's only three," said the owner apologetically. "And I got her from the shelter. I think she's been traumatized by strangers, actually."

"So is this technically a room by New York City law?" said Elinor.

"I don't know," said the girl. "What does that mean?"

"Well, it doesn't have a window," said Elinor. "And for it to be a room under New York City law, it needs a window."

"You can put a fan in there," said the girl, not unpleasantly. "So."

"How much is it?" said Elinor.

"Eleven hundred," said the girl. "Which is honestly a very good rate for the neighborhood. And you get to hang out with this cute little doggie!"

Elinor nodded her head. It was a good rate! It was just so much money there was no way she could possibly swing it.

As Elinor was walking back to the subway, she checked her phone and realized someone had contacted her on Tinder. So far Elinor had gotten no legitimate messages asking her out on a date. She got the occasional communiqué—one message that seemed rather threatening ("Hey girl, lol") and another one from a guy named Sam that was just a winking face but nothing else and she didn't know what to say back.

The guy who'd messaged Elinor was named Jeff. Elinor looked at Jeff's profile. He wasn't holding a dog. In Jeff's profile picture, he was wearing a Barbour jacket and looking out a window so you could only see one side of his face. In another picture, there were five flushed men and Elinor couldn't tell which one was Jeff.

Elinor looked at the message.

"I'm Jeff. Want to get a drink sometime?"

Elinor didn't know if she wanted to get a drink, after going so far on the subway. Was she too tired? To compose her mind, she scanned social media when the train briefly got reception near Wall Street. Out of habit, she immediately checked Mike's Instagram feed, expecting nothing, because Mike was an occasion-based and spasmodic poster. And yet! A mere seventeen minutes before, while Elinor had been stymied underground, Mike had posted a super-blurry filtered photo of Andrea at some kind of party. The picture was just of her long, hopeless face, laughing, crouched over some beer with the label torn off. The caption on the picture just said "#ballers."

Honestly, Elinor was glad that she was going to Mike's mother's Memorial Day party because it was the right thing to do and she had manners, et cetera, et cetera, but she literally couldn't believe that she was the type of person who would happily attend a Memorial Day party out of sheer politesse, and Mike was the type of person who would just callously post a picture of a random girl on his Instagram. It was actually sad that Mike was such an asshole and she was such a polite, kind person who tried and tried to make things civil and normal in an uncivil and nonnormal world.

Perhaps it was good they weren't together if they were such wildly different people. Maybe Mike was always an asshole. Was he? Maybe that was unfair. She wasn't the type of person to spend several years with an asshole. In fact, if she really thought about it and took responsibility, she was the one who had mentioned Andrea in a way that really bothered Mike. Maybe he was posting this picture to hurt her. Maybe that was it. Wow. That was probably it. Maybe he had seen her on Tinder and this was his way to get back at her. How sick and sad, thought Elinor, in a slightly more cheerful frame of mind.

She exited Instagram and went right back to Tinder. So Jeff wanted to meet up? Fine! She wanted to meet up too! Tonight if he was game for it, even though it was 9:15 p.m.

. . .

Elinor found the bar with some trouble. There was no sign out front and no street number. She walked up and down the block three times in increasing confusion. Eventually, she opened the only unmarked door that wasn't a place selling magazines. (Why were there so many places selling magazines? Journalism was in trouble!) It was a nice bar, with very high tin tables and dark lighting and an antique pool table no one was using. It was even peppered with what looked like artsy professionals, tepidly drinking wine. She spotted someone about her age—a kid who vaguely looked like Jeff except a bit shorter and pudgier. A Barbour jacket draped the back of his chair.

"Jeff?" said Elinor to the Jeff-like person. He turned around in his seat, but didn't get up. It was definitely Jeff, if Jeff wore an olive sweater that zipped up halfway.

"Elinor," said Jeff. "Are you Elinor?"

"Yeah," said Elinor. "Hi! Good to meet you."

"Did you have trouble finding the place?"

"A little. But I found it." Jeff looked at her without interest or disinterest. He was drinking a draft beer in a large glass, but was twisting a cocktail straw around one of his fingers like a ring.

"So, how was your day today?" Elinor said.

"Fine," said Jeff. "I'm in town for a conference."

"In town?"

"I usually live in DC, so I'm just like, here for the day. Well, the night and the day."

"Oh," said Elinor. "Do you get up here often?"

"Not that often," said Jeff. "Like, maybe two times a year. I just figured I didn't want to be alone, while I was here. I didn't have anything to do tonight."

"Oh," said Elinor. The nihilism of this sort of depressed her. "I have to go to the bathroom."

"Okay."

Elinor went to the bathroom and just washed her hands.

. . .

"Okay, you can't really see here, but that's Jared, my friend from home."

"Okay," said Elinor. Jeff was showing her a blurry video of some kids at a party. Someone was screaming in a high-pitched voice in the background. Maybe it was Jeff.

"He's just—oh god!" Jeff started laughing. He was having trouble holding the phone steady. "Isn't that super funny?"

"Hahaha," said Elinor. She couldn't really see.

"Let me show you this other thing."

"Okay," said Elinor. Jeff had really bifurcated the evening. First he had talked about his job for a long time. He worked in social networking for some political nonprofit/business organization, but Elinor couldn't really make heads or tails of it. Then he had talked about his friends from home. And then he'd started showing her videos of them. He had shown her these videos for like, twenty minutes.

"So, you said that you like Politico?" said Elinor, desperately. He had said something about Politico twenty minutes ago.

"I said I had a friend that worked there."

"Cool. I actually work for Journalism.ly."

"What's that?" Jeff was looking intently at a video of himself dancing with his friends to a rap song, very badly.

"It's a website," said Elinor. "It's a really fun place to work, I like it a lot."

"Cool," said Jeff. "I haven't heard of it."

"You can look it up!"

"Okay," said Jeff, slightly miffed that Elinor wasn't showing more interest in his videos, perhaps. Jeff dutifully started looking up Journalism.ly on his phone. Elinor saw he clicked on the food fail slide show—which had been the lead story for days.

"What stories did you write? Did you write this one about macadamia nuts?" He gestured to a picture of macadamia nuts and a headline that said "I Had a Reaction to Macadamia Nuts: Here's What You Need to Know."

"No," said Elinor. "Actually, my friend wrote that." That had been performing really well for Nicole, actually.

"Oh cool, my friend works for something like that. Actually she's one of the heads of product design at Yik Yak. She's great. She's like, twenty-three. She does a lot of activisty stuff for them that's kind of changing the way people think about social media from a social perspective? It's cool."

"That's awesome. I'm involved in a really interesting project actually. I try to come up with viral content for the site."

"Like, for the election?"

"No," said Elinor. "Not really. We have this political guy, Josh."

"Sick," said Jeff. There was another pause. Jeff started sword fighting with two cocktail straws.

"Yeah," said Elinor miserably. "Do you want to play pool?"

"Okay," said Jeff.

Jeff abruptly walked over to the pool table, and Elinor followed. Elinor liked pool. She was pretty good at it too. She had had a pool table growing up and had played with her brothers almost daily after school. One time, she and Mike had played pool together and Mike had proceeded to instruct her on various aspects of the game, the spin of the ball, the way that the cue interacted with topspin. Then she beat him, and he actually never played pool with her again after that.

"I'm pretty sick at pool," said Jeff.

"Good," said Elinor. "Me too!"

They started playing. Elinor went first and immediately sank two balls into the left pocket of the table.

While Elinor played, Jeff took out his phone and started texting on it.

"Ha-ha," he laughed.

"What's going on with your phone?"

"I'll show you after. My friend sent me this super funny thing."

"Oh, ha-ha," said Elinor.

Jeff was terrible at pool. He couldn't even get one ball in.

Elinor took another turn and sank three more balls in great concentration.

"Your turn," said Elinor.

"Uh, hold on." Jeff was texting, hunched over his phone, which was casting a dull blue light on his face.

"We can just sit down," said Elinor. "If you'd rather."

"Yeah," said Jeff. "Sorry, pool's boring, I think."

"I thought you said you were good at it."

"I am. I just don't feel like it right now."

Elinor felt very tired all of a sudden.

"You know what," said Elinor. "I'm going to go." It was fifty-nine minutes in. She had done her duty.

" 'K," said Jeff, jerking his head up. "Text me later if you want to meet up. It was good to meet you. Let me know how that journalism thing goes."

"Will do!" said Elinor. She hugged him with the top front of her body and took a cab home. On the way home, Jeff texted, "lmk if you want to meet up later." She didn't respond.

. . .

Elinor's life hobbled on—a maimed animal plodding down a country road—with occasional respites. For one, she found an apartment on Craigslist. It was nine hundred dollars a month. And it was a studio! In Astoria, sort of! It didn't have a bathroom or a kitchen or a sink, but that was fine. She just had to share a hall bathroom with the landlord, who was a very old woman. And she could buy a hot plate, which was a lot like a kitchen. Eventually, she would move into a real apartment in Brooklyn, but in the meantime, she could stop interviewing to be someone's roommate. She was starting to hate all of these traumatized dogs who couldn't stop barking. But that made her feel like a bad person.

At work one day, Elinor was finishing up a story called "The 10 Things Any Woman Doesn't Want to Hear on a Date"—the first one was "Look at this video of my friend from home"—when Peter walked up to her.

"Hey, Elinor," said Peter. "I'm just checking in with you. What are you working on? The Vans sneakers list didn't do that well and I just want to help you make this piece a real blockbuster, so let me know if there is anything I can do to help."

"J.W. told me to do the Vans sneakers one," said Elinor.

"He did?" said Peter. "But he's on partnerships."

"I know. But he's my mentor. Or he said he was my mentor? Whatever that means. I don't really get it." Elinor hadn't seen J.W. since their talk. When she had emailed him her Vans sneakers story, he didn't respond. He had bought a large blind for one of the glass walls of the conference room so you couldn't see in anymore.

"J.W. is your mentor?" said Peter.

"I mean, I don't know. I guess so?"

"I guess a person can have two mentors."

"Or one mentor," said Elinor. "Or no mentors."

"And one of the problems with women in the workforce is that they say that older men don't really mentor younger women because everyone finds it really creepy," said Peter. He had a sad look on his face again. "But you actually have two male mentors! Which just says a lot about the values this place has."

"But what if like, I don't even want a mentor or anything?"

"I should talk to J.W. about what he's mentoring you about, so that we don't overlap on what we mentor. What did you think about my idea that I emailed you today? When are you going to start working on that?"

" 'Ten Things Breast Cancer Awareness Month Does'? I'll get to it after I finish this thing. Like, five minutes."

"Okay, but get on it. I think it could be huge."

Privately Elinor didn't agree.

"But, even though I'm mentoring you about this, I won't be able to be that involved. Tim just quit. So I have a lot more work now."

"Who is Tim?" Elinor still didn't really know anybody at the Journalism.ly because no one ever talked or introduced themselves or went out after work. She knew only Nicole.

"Tim? Maybe J.W. can introduce you to him in his capacity as mentor. Tim did product design and he's leaving to start an online zine about SoulCycle. J.W. was really upset about it, because he's the fifth person to quit this month."

"Well, I have to do something even worse than working," said Elinor.

"What's that?" said Peter.

"I have to move on Saturday." Elinor was really not looking forward to moving. She still had three days left in her apartment and she was treasuring them. She hadn't even put anything in boxes yet. She bought boxes though. They were sitting in a flat pile near her bathtub-shower and they were getting a little wet because water kept splattering on them, and yet still, Elinor had not moved them to a safer location.

"Where are you moving to?" asked Peter.

"Queens."

"Roommates?"

"No," said Elinor. "It's like a studio. And then there is this bathroom out in the hall."

"Why don't you move to Brooklyn?" said Peter. "That's where I live."

"I know," said Elinor. "I would have."

"Brooklyn's great. There are all these coffee shops. And such cool people. You should move there."

"That sounds great," said Elinor, feeling like a loser. It was very typical of her to somehow not live in the place where all of the zeitgeist was happening. "I actually really wanted to move to Brooklyn. I'm still going to. This is just a transitional place. I was having trouble finding roommates. And sometimes I feel like I'm actually too old to have Craigslist roommates? Well, I guess I sort of have a roommate still—"

"Do you have anyone to help you move?"

"Uh, no. I don't. But it's not that much stuff. I don't even have a bed."

"What do you sleep on?" asked Peter.

"Ha-ha, I was just joking," said Elinor, now embarrassed about the foam pad. "It's basically a futon, which is like a bed. Anyway, I just don't have a frame. It's not hard to move."

"Where's Mike?" asked Peter.

"Um." Elinor knew this moment had to arrive at some point. It was odd to her, however, that she still had no real narrative for any of it. "We're kind of not together anymore."

"A break?" said Peter.

"Yeah. It's okay. We're still really good friends. He's just going through some stuff right now." Elinor thought of Andrea's face, in profile like a Pre-Raphaelite painting, and quickly dismissed it.

"Oh," said Peter. His eyes had the frozen look of someone who had wandered into a closet where people were arguing.

"I still really respect Mike," said Elinor. "He's such a good guy and an amazing friend."

Peter nodded, and his visible fear dissipated slightly.

"Well, if you want I can help you."

"Help what?"

"Move."

"Oh my god," said Elinor. "You don't have to do that."

"I do have to work that day, but I can definitely help you. I should be done at the office around two p.m."

"Uh, thanks," said Elinor. Idly, she wondered if Peter was even in love with her. However, every single time Elinor thought someone was in love with her, he never ever was. Like, that really skinny guy she dated in college who seemed to have no feeling toward her at all. It was surprising, at the time, how much this hurt Elinor's feelings, and perhaps she could attribute the sting to the element of surprise. Before they slept together, she was convinced she was doing him a special favor he would never forget. He was always looking at her across the room. When they actually did have sex, he seemed to be floating above his body, his eyes screwed shut. He never spoke to her again after they finally did it. He dated someone else senior year. Sometimes Elinor looked her up on Facebook.

"Okay, see you then!" said Peter, a bit too enthusiastically. He went back to his desk.

. . .

It was 2:14 p.m. when Peter arrived at her door to help her move. Elinor was slightly annoyed at herself, and oddly also at Peter for his appearance. She still hadn't done much packing. She had put one or two posters in a box that wasn't totally taped together. She had removed the shower curtain and fully exposed the bathtub—which was a mistake. There was still all this brown stuff on the bottom of the bathtub from when they moved in. Seeing it decontextualized, it looked embarrassing. What the hell was it? And did they somehow cause it?

She hadn't actually thought that Peter was going to come help her move anyway. The offer had seemed like one of those empty things people say and don't do. But he had texted last night asking her what time he was supposed to arrive. She said 2:00 but then she slept in until 1:47. So fuck Peter.

When Elinor opened the door for Peter (after two minutes of looking at herself in the mirror, dazed, her hair forming a pyramid), he hugged her with one arm. Luckily it was brief. Elinor led him into the apartment.

"How was work?"

Peter looked around circumspectly. She saw he saw the wet boxes.

"Fine," said Peter.

"What did you do?"

"A bunch of shit. I don't know. J.W. sent me kind of a weird email last night."

"Oh," said Elinor. "Why was it weird?"

"Well, Sean was cc'd," said Peter, who leaned against the

single cabinet that happened to make up Elinor's kitchen and looked down at the floor. "So it was really bad. Because Sean was mad that we hadn't put up this viral Vine that everyone's talking about. You know that one of that kid who eats a glow stick and then his eyes glow?"

"No," said Elinor.

"Yeah, apparently, everyone's obsessed with it. And someone showed it to Sean this weekend and he was like, mad that we didn't have it on our site. He emailed me and J.W. about it."

"Oh."

"Yeah, and then I chimed in and was like, 'I'll have it up shortly,' and J.W. was like, 'Peter, you should really be on top of breaking Vines, we need Vines to be more systematic,' which would have been fine if Sean wasn't cc'd but he was cc'd, so it was so awkward. It was like I wasn't on top of breaking Vines, when that's not even my job. I'm trying to get our Music.ly ready for the election!"

"Ugh, that sucks," said Elinor. "Is he trying to mentor you or something?"

"No. J.W. really doesn't understand how swamped I am. Still, he's a brilliant writer," said Peter in a change of tone, as if, suddenly, he was composing the eulogy for J.W.'s funeral. "So what do you want me to move?"

"Well, uh, I guess you should start with some of these smaller boxes of kitchen stuff. I'll wrap up some of the stuff in the desk and start packing that. I don't have a bed, so the desk is probably it, really."

"Okay," said Peter, nicely not mentioning the foam pad. He opened up Elinor's one cabinet and started putting things into a box. He did this in silence for ten minutes.

"What do you think of J.W.?" he said, abruptly.

"I don't know. He's fine."

"I just feel like we should really delegate someone else to be on breaking Vines," said Peter with unexpected vitriol, slamming a box on top of another box. "Because that person is not me. I am so overloaded from tweeting, and from my own writing."

"Yeah." Elinor hoped that box didn't have plates in it, because it sounded like it did.

"I mean, from now on I'm going to be on top of Vines more. But I also think we should hire a Vine person. Sean is right that we shouldn't miss stuff like that because Vines are important."

"If you say so," said Elinor. "Should I start a Vine account? Are you on Vine?"

"No," said Peter. "I mean, I have an account but I don't use it."

For the next two hours (Elinor had no idea it was going to take so long, but somehow it did; apparently, she had a lot of stuff) Peter moved Elinor out of her apartment.

It was hard work. Peter completely disassembled the desk. He scraped poster gum off the walls. He wrapped several forks individually in newspaper. Throughout the move, he was mostly silent, and after some abortive attempts at conversation, Elinor was too. It was when they got off the subway with the first group of boxes that he started to speak in earnest. Elinor was having trouble with her box; it kept slipping out of her hands, it seemed to be covered in a slick of dust.

"So what's the deal with you and Mike?" he said abruptly. This was not what Elinor was expecting Peter to say, especially after how much it had seemed to upset his humors the last time.

"The deal?" Elinor juggled her box. "It's complicated. Why?"

"No reason," said Peter. "I'm just wondering."

"I mean, did Mike tell you anything at all about it? Has he been talking about it with everyone? Is that why you ask?"

"No, no." Peter looked off into space. "Mike and I actually don't talk very much."

"Oh. I thought you did."

"No. We're both really busy. I should get a drink with him actually. I'd love to hear about Memo Points Daily."

"Okay." Then Elinor decided to say something she had been thinking in such a constant refrain that she almost felt she had said it at some point before. "Is he seeing someone else? He's allowed to," she added quickly. "I won't be mad if you tell me."

"I really don't know." Peter stared at his box. "I said I don't talk to him that much."

"But just if you've seen him? That was all I meant. If you had seen him, maybe."

"I didn't."

They walked along in silence.

Eventually, Peter and Elinor got to her new apartment. It was a brick building with small, arcane windows like a power plant's. They were greeted at the door by Elinor's landlord, Kathy, a tiny woman with a grizzled face.

"I was wondering when you'd show up," she said.

"Hahaha," said Elinor. "I'm sorry, I know I said four and it's four-thirty."

"Next time, tell me if you are going to be moving late into the night. I don't have all day. Here is the key."

"Thank you," said Elinor. "This is my friend Peter."

"Nice to meet you," said Kathy "I'll show you up to the room."

They walked up four flights to a small, dark door in the back of the building.

"You didn't tell me it was a walk-up," said Peter in a whisper.

"I'm sorry," said Elinor, quietly.

"Now, I don't want you using the bathroom at all hours of the night. We share a wall," said the landlord. "And it's a very sensitive toilet."

"It's probably going to be way better than being in the basement though," Peter kept whispering. "Way more light."

"It doesn't actually have *that* much more light," said Elinor, "which is kind of funny."

"Okay, this key unlocks the top lock, this one unlocks the bottom lock. It's a very temperamental key, so just jiggle it," said Kathy. She was still mad, obviously.

"Okay," said Elinor.

"Use your own towels. Don't use my towels."

"I won't," said Elinor. "I would never do that. Thanks so much, Kathy."

Kathy shrugged and went back into her apartment.

Elinor pried the door open. It was a very small room—having Peter in there was a bit too much for it. There was only one window, very high on the wall, like a porthole in a ship's cabin.

"Is your desk going to fit?" asked Peter.

. . .

"Well, that's the last of it," Peter announced.

"Thank you so much," said Elinor. She was sweating into her tank top's built-in bra.

"It's fine," said Peter, looking around her apartment again. They'd had to leave the desk on the street, so it was just a foam pad and some books. Her clothes were still in her suitcase because there wasn't a closet. Elinor needed to get one of those fabric-covered hanger things.

"Do you want to get pizza?" said Elinor. "I'll take you out. I owe you hugely for helping me move."

"No," said Peter. "I really don't need anything. I'm okay. I've got to go."

"Really? I feel so bad. Do you want money?" Elinor had taken out cash. She went over to her purse and started rifling through it.

Peter squinted at her. "That's okay. Seriously. I've got so much work. We both do actually."

"Okay," said Elinor. "Well, thank you so much!"

"It's fine." Peter waved to her without looking at her and left. He seemed a bit upset, but Elinor didn't know why. She didn't care really either.

. . .

The next day, Elinor lay in bed, the back of her T-shirt adhering to the foam pad. She heard a dim rush of water emanate from the wall. She was probably near the bathroom pipes—she heard a constant rushing that sometimes intensified but never really stopped.

Elinor rolled to her other side and looked at her phone—a tiny pink square with a cracked screen. Her phone said she had a text. Maybe it was Mike, worried about her now transient life.

It was from Jeff.

Have you seen this? Rofl

It was a link to a viral Vine of the kid who ate a glow stick and then his eyes glowed.

Chapter 8

Facebook: 1 post: A selfie of Elinor clad in some kind of span-dex horror that indicates she has recently been to the gym. Comment: "In troubling, polarizing times, it is important to take time for yourself and remember who you are outside of the polit-ical circus. That is why I did yoga last night. Thanks so much to the people at @gangstersweat. You guys make yoga fun and you really helped with my self-care!" Thirty likes.

Twitter: 28 tweets. Sample: "When things are hard that just means you have to work harder at it —Robert Frost."

Instagram: 2 pictures. The first seems to be taken out the win-dow of a moving vehicle. It is night. All you can see are blurry swirling lights. Caption: "#nighthawks." Five likes, because, hon-estly, what the fuck.

The second is a selfie with a granulated, washed-out filter on it. Elinor is smirking, mouth closed. Her shirt is slightly low cut. She is holding the camera above her. Possibly she is lying on the foam pad even though you can't really see that. Caption: "Mood =" and then an emoji of painting nails. Twenty-two likes.

Snapchat: Elinor takes a video of herself using a new filter that makes her eyes even larger and her mouth even smaller.

. . .

Hey," said Elinor. "This is cool. I've never done something like this before."

"Yeah," said Will. "I went here for a picnic once." He was holding a coffee. Elinor was in love with him, she thought, maybe. In some lights, he was sort of handsome. In others, he looked like all the features of his face were slowly sliding off his skin.

"Yes!" said Elinor. It was 11:00 a.m. and they were walking along some abandoned train tracks that ran trippingly down a muddy embankment. Occasionally, Elinor would see a luminescent milk jug in a puddle of water. Later they were going to go to a coffee shop to do a crossword puzzle. Elinor was cold and she had gotten mud on the top of her sneaker and it was seeping into her foot. She should have worn boots.

Elinor had met Will on a dating site she was on called HowAboutWe. HowAboutWe had dates that were actually activities. Will had suggested "How About We Walk Around Abandoned Train Tracks and Then Get a Coffee and Do the Crossword," and Elinor had taken Will up on that offer because she had done the crossword with Mike occasionally and it was pretty fun.

"So, you work at a start-up you were saying?" said Elinor.

"Yeah, it's an advertising start-up."

"I work for a start-up too, that's so interesting—"

"I'm working with these two guys, Darren and Jonah. I do

more of the front-end stuff. Darren and Jonah are more of the back-end people. Essentially they are programming the site. And I'm kind of the one getting our partnerships, making our calls, things like that."

"That's so interesting," said Elinor. "I definitely don't work at the back end of my job either."

"Yeah, don't get me wrong, we need programmers. But programmers can be more on the narrow-minded end of the spectrum. Steve Jobs never programmed, you know? I feel like I'm the one making more of the big strategic decisions, which is where I like to be anyway, so it's a perfect fit."

"I actually come up with viral content for my job. Is that what you guys do?"

"Sort of," said Will. "There's a bit more to it than that."

"I work at Journalism.ly. I do the viral content there. Have you heard of it?"

"No," said Will. "But I have a lot of friends that work in journalism. My ex-girlfriend, well, maybe not 'ex-girlfriend' but the girl I was seeing at one point last year, worked in journalism and I used to hang out with her friends all the time. I didn't really like her friends. I mean, she was great but her friends sucked. They seemed really full of themselves."

"I don't think journalists are full of themselves," said Elinor. "At all. I think we all just take our jobs really seriously."

"Yeah, these people were full of themselves though. I don't know. I got a bad impression."

There was a pause, as Elinor tried to get over how suddenly offended she got on behalf of all journalists, writ large. She took several seconds to compose herself.

"How much longer is the walk?" she asked. Elinor realized

she was very cold, or at least, the tips of her fingers were. She wasn't wearing gloves. Also her wet feet.

"Not much longer," said Will. "We're almost at this coffee shop. It's like, right near my apartment."

"That's convenient," said Elinor. Were they going to have sex at 11:30 a.m.? That was novel.

About five minutes later, Elinor and Will got to the coffee shop. It looked a bit like a 1950s diner. The menu was displayed on a large black board that had grooves in it, and white plastic letters hung off the grooves. Some of the letters were crooked, but it looked like that was on purpose. Will and Elinor both got coffees and paid for them separately, and even though Elinor was hungry and wanted a muffin, she didn't get one because she didn't know Will wasn't going to pay for her until after she ordered her coffee. Not that it wasn't fine for Will to not pay for her—it was totally fine. It was better because she actually liked paying for herself, but she wished she had known that.

After some listless standing, they finally sat at a small, round marble table in the corner of the coffee shop. This was lucky because the entire coffee shop was teeming with people. Two people elbowed Elinor in line.

"That guy just elbowed me in line," said Elinor. "Can you believe that?"

"It's really crowded in here," said Will.

"Yeah, I guess so," said Elinor. "But still, you know?"

Will didn't answer her. He took out his *Times* from where he was holding it in the pocket of his jacket and tossed it on the table. Elinor sat down and put her coat on the back of her chair. Will took a ballpoint pen out of his pocket and wrote down two answers quickly, as Elinor sipped her coffee.

"Okay," said Elinor. She decided to insert herself. "Five letters. 'Place to be in the hot seat'? Uh, I don't know, the tub?"

"That's not five letters."

"Tubs?"

"That's four letters."

Will thought.

"It's 'sauna,'" he said.

"'Sauna'? Oh my god. You are totally right. 'Sauna.' Why didn't I think of that? That's so brilliant."

"'Amtrak guests for short,'" said Will. "Three letters."

"'Train,'" said Elinor. "Ha-ha, no, that's not three letters. Um, hmm, let me see? Hmm. 'Tren'?"

"I think it's 'ETA.'"

"Oh my god. Estimated time of arrival. That's exactly it. God, I used to be so good at these. I haven't done this in a while. I'm rusty! And I am actually a writer for a living, okay? Like, I majored in this shit, I should know this."

They did the crossword together like this for a while. Elinor went to the bathroom in the middle. Will didn't really speak much during the crossword, he really wanted to *do* the crossword. And he mostly wanted to do it by himself. When she and Mike did the crossword it wasn't so horribly businesslike. Mike would often indulge himself in spirited digressions about various clues.

After another thirty minutes or so, Will had finished about half of the crossword puzzle. He sighed audibly.

"That was a hard one today. I usually get more than half. Jesus."

"Well, at least it kept you busy," snapped Elinor. "We didn't really talk." She laughed in a forced way. Then realized what she had done. Fuck! She'd probably just snapped at him because she was mad at herself for not doing well at crossword puzzles. What was the matter with her?

"Well, hmm, it was really nice to meet you," said Will, seemingly slightly put off by her outburst and rising out of his seat. "Not everyone would just walk along some railroad tracks in the middle of Brooklyn."

"Ha-ha," said Elinor. "Well, if they don't, they are crazy. That was an amazing idea for a date."

"Yeah," said Will. He already had his coat on.

"I had a great time," said Elinor, overcompensating for snapping. "I actually love stuff like this. This is my ideal date."

"Cool, well, see you around?"

"Yeah!" said Elinor. This was, in many ways, the best date she had ever been on, aside from the fact that she'd snapped at Will. Maybe Will was just kind of hard to get to know. That didn't bother Elinor. In fact, she *liked* guys who were hard to get to know. She liked to put effort in.

"We'll see," said Will. "Bye."

They both walked out of the coffee shop and Will stood on the corner as she crossed the street. She realized that Will was going into the building where the coffee shop was through a separate glass door that led to a series of apartments. So his apartment was actually in the coffee shop? Elinor was momentarily piqued at Will's transportation convenience. She had to take two subways to get back to Queens. This feeling immediately subsided into guilt. Elinor was always surprised by how socially inappropriate she could be at times.

. . .

"I hope he calls me," said Elinor. "I just don't know if snapping at him was a big deal or not." She was walking with Sheila up Thirty-second Street. They had just had brunch at a diner near Sheila's apartment. So far, Sheila had not been out to Queens and visited Elinor at her apartment, which was so typical, but Elinor wasn't going to say anything about it.

"Well, how long has it been?" said Sheila.

"Like, a week. But we actually had a pretty good date, I'm surprised he hasn't texted. Do you think it's because I snapped at him?"

"I bet he's just busy at work or something." Sheila's tone betrayed a slight boredom. They had talked about this for most of the brunch, but not in a particularly satisfying way, in Elinor's opinion. Sheila, when distracted, always sort of acted like it was your fault when something bad happened to you.

"But what about you?" said Elinor, magnanimously. "I feel like we haven't really discussed Ralph at all."

"I'm seeing him tonight. We're going to go to the movies."

"What are you wearing?"

"That cream sweater I have and my jeans and those boots I have that have the buckles on them."

"Cute," said Elinor. "I love that sweater."

"I don't think it's the sweater you are thinking of. I got a new cream sweater that I think you haven't seen. I got it for Christmas. It has this high neck, and kind of like cutouts. I can't tell if it's too much."

"I bet it's not," said Elinor. "I bet it's really cute."

"I hope so," said Sheila, doubtfully. "Anyway, Ralph's been

really nice lately. Ever since my birthday, I told you, he's been texting me a lot more and stuff and kind of like, being way nicer. We have more of a friend vibe right now. Like, we're actually friends now. It's really nice."

"That's good," said Elinor.

"Yeah, I think he's really changed. And like, our relationship is so much more normal. He was actually talking about like, moving in?"

"What? To your apartment?"

"Um, yeah!" said Sheila. "Because like, Caroline is going to move out. She just told us like, two days ago. She just got a job in Seattle. And I was texting Ralph about it, and Ralph was like, Well, I need a new place. Is that room free? And I was like, Yes? But like, then I was like, Why do you want to know! And he was like, Well what if I moved in? Kind of like a joke? But then we actually talked about it more and he was like, Well I am actually looking for a place, and then I told him about the room, and then—"

"Wait, what?" said Elinor. "Ralph is moving in with you and all of your friends? That seems like a really bad idea."

"I don't actually think it is," said Sheila. "I mean, I get why you are saying it's a bad idea, but like, you don't really get how we're actually friends now. I know you are like, rolling your eyes, but you really have to believe me. There is nothing between us. It's weird, I know. But it's been really great. It's been really relaxing—"

"Are the other girls okay with it?"

"I think so. I mean, they said they'd be okay with a guy roommate. I don't think they'd be okay with it if we were like, dating because I see how that could be a little bit weird? But since we're not. I mean, it's not like I'm moving in with my boyfriend, and they all know that."

"Um, okay?" said Elinor. She walked along in silence. This was the stupidest idea, ever. Ralph and Sheila were never just friends, and this was surely going to end in tears. And another thing—how come Sheila, who was supposed to be her best friend, invited Ralph into her apartment—but not Elinor? Elinor could have taken Caroline's space. Elinor had just had to move to Queens! And it did suck there. Her landlady-roommate was in the bathroom constantly.

Sheila seemed to sense this sentiment, even though Elinor didn't say anything. She glanced at her, head tilted to the side.

"You know I would have invited you, right? But Caroline like, *just* told us, and then I was talking to Ralph and Ralph and I became so platonic—"

"In the space of a week?"

"Like, way longer than that. Like a month!"

That was a lie, but Elinor, at this point, was far too tired to refute it. She could have brought out text evidence, however, that directly rebutted this time line.

"Anyway, you know I would rather live with you, right?" said Sheila. "You know that, right?"

"All right, all right," said Elinor. "But, Sheila, honestly, separate from me, we aren't actually talking about me here. You have to really think about whether this is what you want and whether you can handle it."

"I can handle it," said Sheila, tremulously.

"I really wonder if you can," said Elinor. "It just seems so dumb. How do you know whether—"

"Listen, I don't want to talk about it anymore," said Sheila. "Can we just talk about something else?"

They continued down the street wordlessly, two friends of long standing on a promenade of Park Avenue.

. . .

The next day, Elinor was at work. She happened to be in a terrible mood. Will had not called her or texted, even though she had texted Will and said, "I know this isn't what I'm supposed to do, but I don't really care what I'm supposed to do. Had a really great time the other morning." At first she thought that such a text showed the kind of person she was—a woman who flouted conventions—but now she really hated that she had done it.

In order to distract herself, she had spent the day scrolling through her various social media accounts. She wondered what kind of person other people thought she was. If she died, for example, and only her social media accounts survived for Mike to read at her funeral, what would everyone think? She wanted people to see her as beautiful and moral, warmhearted and historically correct, extremely tolerant but able to call out wrongdoing when she saw it, aware of all possible holes in her thinking, not defensive except when provoked, mildly irreverent but then unexpectedly sincere about the possibility of the American experiment. In short, she wanted to be perceived how everyone else wanted to be perceived in her small circle of digital friends. Luckily, this is one of the easier personalities in the world to pretend that you have.

Yet Elinor also wanted something else, slightly more complicated—she wanted people to know she was suffering. She wanted them to see that beneath her wide-eyed self-portraits and urban panoramas, she had been abandoned by an adventurer. Were they fully comprehending the quiet bravery in her position? It was hard to know.

It was in this meditative state of mind that she saw Mike had tweeted something he wrote for Memo Points Daily. It was a long think piece called "Why the World Needs to Think Seriously About Iran and Why It Hasn't and Why, Maybe, It Can't."

Elinor saw that the piece had seventy-seven favorites on Twitter. Seventy-seven! And it wasn't just from randoms, like Elinor's pieces often were favorited by. In fact, she saw all these people of note complimenting Mike, as if he were winning an award. "Great piece from my friend Mike_Moriarty_Journo," the actual Richard Cooley had tweeted, cartoon and all!

How were he and Mike friends? Did they meet at work? Would he be attending the Memorial Day party? She closed Twitter, and to make herself feel better, she chatted Nicole on Slack.

"Ugh," typed Elinor. "Did you see Mike wrote a piece?" She copied and pasted the link to Nicole.

"Yeah," typed Nicole. "I'm just over men and their think pieces. I mean, that's literally what male privilege is."

"You are so right," said Elinor. "I don't know, it's just so hard to be a feminist right now. You should see what my friend Sheila is doing? She's moving in with this guy who has been treating her like shit for six years. But like, supposedly they are just 'friends.'"

"Well we all have been there," typed Nicole. "But that is so fucked up and pathetic."

"I know," typed Elinor. "I'm really sad about it for her. Honestly, I'm going to try and not look at Mike's stuff for a while. I think that's better for me."

"Totally. That's self-care."

Elinor became aware of Peter standing over her. He was talking to her. She took her headphones off.

"Peter, what?"

"Did you see that Mike wrote that piece?" Peter was wearing a plaid shirt today. It was red and black checkered.

"Yes. I did."

"Good piece," said Peter, ruminatively.

"Peter, did you literally just come here to tell me my exboyfriend wrote a good piece? What is the matter with you!"

"Seriously, Peter? You are such a troll," said Nicole. Elinor didn't know she was listening, but she was, she had her headphones off.

"I'm not a troll," said Peter.

"You are a troll," said Elinor.

"You are always trolling Elinor and you need to stop," said Nicole.

"I'm not a troll," said Peter, stubbornly. "I'm actually coming here to check in on the breast cancer awareness piece."

"I put up the piece already. It didn't do that well." To be honest, Elinor had been a little bit disappointed by the performance of her last couple of pieces. Every single one she did on the request of her mentors did terribly. She was getting to understand what made a piece viral or not. At the very least, the subject matter had to be sort of fun or interesting.

"I think it's just because you didn't push it enough. You should have been tweeting it every hour. Also, I don't appreciate you guys calling me a troll, that's not appropriate. And if you clear something with J.W., you should clear it with me!"

"Well, technically, I don't have to clear it with anyone?" said Elinor. But Peter didn't hear her. He had wandered away.

. . .

"That's really shitty," said Nicole. They were both holding coffees and walking slowly up the stairs.

"I know," said Elinor. She sighed loudly. "I just don't know what to do! I keep going on these dates and they all blow. No one even wants to make out. My ex is writing all this awesome shit about Iran."

"Did you read it?" said Nicole.

"Yes," said Elinor. She had read the first couple of lines. "And it's amazing. I mean, at least I'm happy I dated someone so smart, you know? I was maybe going to read it and be like, Hey, this is really good. Just to be nice. Because I feel like that's probably a good thing, or whatever, since he works in journalism."

"Do you want to come out with me and my friends tonight?" said Nicole.

"I'd love to," said Elinor. She smiled. This was going to be the first time she was going to hang out with Nicole outside of the confines of work. She really liked Nicole. Talking to Nicole was pretty much exactly how she thought talking should go, theoretically.

"We're going to this magazine party. It's probably going to be awful—"

"Oh shit," said Elinor. "I promised I would get a drink with my friend Sheila tonight, even though I'm kind of pissed at her honestly."

"Bring her!" said Nicole. "The more the merrier."

"I'll see," said Elinor. When Elinor got back to her table, she texted Sheila a confusing message that was, on the face of it, a tepid invitation to attend Nicole's party, but was, in actuality, a plea for Sheila to reschedule their hangout. Sheila, however, refused to understand the subtext. She texted back that she would be extremely excited to hang out with Nicole, and told Elinor she would be happy to accompany her to the party. Elinor comforted herself with the thought that she was a very good person, and Sheila was lucky to have her as a friend.

Chapter 9

Facebook: 1 post: "What an inspiring, important article! Especially in these polarizing times. Great job Mike Moriarty [hyperlinked]." Attached is Mike's article about Iran, which is not particularly inspiring actually, but instead rather strident. Elinor hadn't read the whole thing. Ten likes, but no like from Mike Moriarty, the object.

Twitter: Dull, some aggrieved spats, some quotations. Not worth repeating.

Instagram: 1 photo: An expansive snap of the tops of several people's heads and a person reading in the middle of the room. Caption: "Reading at @redhookartspace #RichardCooleyIsKillingIt."

. . .

The party was being held in some cavernous loft space. White Christmas lights were twirled around the scaffolding that held up the ceiling and large, square windows looked out on a bleak vista of other identical warehouses used for similar events. The room was packed with people—all clad in various noncolors and T-shirts, a hum of talk emanating from each of their groups like static from a speaker.

"I'm going to get a drink," said Elinor to Nicole, who was hanging her coat on a rack and texting with one thumb.

"Me too," said Nicole. "My friends say they're near the bar."

"Great. I really need a drink, I think. What a shitty day."

As Elinor and Nicole walked toward the bar (which was wooden and free-standing, as if they had rolled it in like a coffin at a wake), Elinor scanned the room for Mike. It wouldn't be shocking if he was here. He was a writer. Elinor couldn't see him, however, in all the haircuts she scanned.

After Elinor and Nicole ordered their drinks (two bitter glasses of white wine) Nicole spotted her friends. One girl with a bobbed haircut and square black spectacles and another girl wearing a sailor shirt. The girl in the stripes waved to Nicole.

"Hey, guys," said Nicole. "This is Elinor."

"Oh, hey," said the striped girl. "I'm Gretchen."

"I'm sorry to drag you out here," said the girl in the glasses.

"There's like, no one here," said Gretchen. Some guy hip-checked Gretchen because he was walking very quickly toward the bar, and so as a group, they clutched their wines and migrated three feet to the left.

"Should we go somewhere else?" said Nicole.

"I mean, I guess we should stay for the reading?" said the glasses girl. "It would be a little rude if we left."

"Okay," said Nicole. She took out her phone and started looking at it, and so Elinor took out her phone and started looking at it. Nothing was happening on Elinor's phone. No one had texted her and no one had updated Instagram since she last used it. She started looking at this news app, but she had already read all the stories. In her whole life, she had never been so caught up on the ephemera of what was happening in the world and the microdiscussions those things engendered.

"Did you see that thing Charmaine wrote?" asked the girl in the glasses, in the direction of Nicole. "We were just talking about it before you guys got here."

"I did. That was so crazy," said Nicole.

"I mean, it's brave for her to write about her abortion, but she didn't have to criticize her ex so much. I know him and I don't think that's right."

"I think anyone has the right to write anything. We can't criticize her experience," said Nicole, expansively. "At the same time, I felt like she was kind of deaf to how privileged it seemed. A lot of people don't have access to abortion or the money for it."

"I think you are right," said Gretchen. "Anyone can write about anything however they want to. But it was really weird how she did it, I think? It was like she was the only person who ever got an abortion. I don't know."

"Yeah," said Glasses Girl. "Also Jim just walked in."

"Who's Jim?" said Elinor.

"Jim is this guy Elise was seeing," said Nicole, gesturing to the girl in the glasses.

"He was a super nice guy, we both weren't ready for anything," said Elise. "He had just gotten out of something and I wanted to be single. But then I sent him a sext and he didn't respond? So I got really pissed."

"That sucks," said Elinor.

"I just don't know whether to say hi to him or not because of the sext."

"Do whatever you want, I think," said Elinor. "I think you can't do the wrong thing. Like, I just congratulated my ex on Facebook for an article he wrote. And at first I was like, Why am I doing this? but then I realized I can do what I want, and it was actually a really nice openhearted thing for me to compliment him on Facebook."

"Who's your ex?" said Elise.

"Mike Moriarty. He works for Memo Points Daily?"

"Oh, I've heard of him. I think?"

"His mom is Pam Johnson."

"Oh yeah, yeah, I think I know of him. Cool. Why did you guys break up?"

"Oh, I don't know," said Elinor. "Basically he had these people over at the house and I fell asleep and he got really mad at me and then he broke up with me. Well, it was mutual, kind of. But I was a little surprised."

"That's so dick," said Elise. "How long did you guys date?"

"Four years."

"Wow, that is insanely dick."

"Yeah," said Elinor. "I guess it is dick. He made me feel really guilty about falling asleep."

"Elise works for Buzzle," said Nicole helpfully, before looking at her phone again.

"How cool," said Elinor. Buzzle was a website that Elinor read all the time. In many ways, it was similar to Journalism.ly, but it was also a little bit different in a way Elinor couldn't quite put into words.

"Yeah, I love it," said Elise. "I'm working on a piece about how Taylor Swift is kind of like Amazing Amy from *Gone Girl* and how that's really bad for women."

"Oh yeah?" said Elinor, feeling a pang of jealousy. Sometimes it was so embarrassing to say she was responsible for a very viral list. She wasn't necessarily a cultural commentator like everyone else. She didn't write think pieces, like Mike, or Nicole or Peter even. She decided to change the subject. "You know, it's interesting that you say Mike is a dick. Maybe he was."

"Legit. I bet he's just one of those broey journalist assholes. My ex was one of those. But now I'm at Buzzle so fuck him."

"Yeah, maybe," said Elinor, warming to her theme. "And now he's like, always with this other girl on Instagram. But she's really annoying. Her Instagram is like, literally just annoying landscapes. She thinks she's amazing."

"Ugh, vom!" said Elise. "I think I'm going to write an essay about all the things you can learn from someone's Instagram. Okay, I'm going to text Jim now and tell him I saw him so if we run into each other he just knows that I'm here." Elise stood over her phone and started texting.

Next to them, Nicole was talking to Gretchen about an OkCupid date.

"He's nice," said Gretchen, "but look at these texts." Nicole bent her head over the texts and Elinor stared at her own phone, willing it to update with something, which was when Sheila texted her that she was outside and needed Elinor to get her. Elinor felt a shiver of annoyance, which was irrational because she had just texted Sheila to see where she was.

Elinor walked out of the warehouse without her coat on. It

was very windy, and Elinor's blouse whipped against her like a flag. She saw Sheila shambling around the corner, eventually.

"Hey," said Sheila, breathless. "Sorry I'm late."

"It's no big deal," said Elinor. "But let's get inside though."

"What is this thing again?" asked Sheila, passing through a dark vestibule where two people were talking to each other in a dull corner. "I just had the worst day. You won't believe what happened to me. Remember that girl, Megan, that I was telling you about?"

"Uh-huh," said Elinor, scanning the room for Nicole and her friends. They had moved. Where were they? Elinor saw Nicole and Gretchen finally, in the line for the bathroom. She started walking toward them, quickly.

"Anyway, Megan like, wants to take over my shifts? And had talked to the supervisor about it? I was so pissed because I finally had stopped working all the time on the weekends, and now like, she's trying to take that away from me? I literally almost cried in front of the supervisor."

"That sucks," said Elinor. They had almost approached Nicole and Gretchen.

"Hey, guys," said Elinor, to the both of them. "Are you in line for the bathroom?"

"Yeah," said Nicole. "It's a really long line."

"So this is my friend Sheila," said Elinor.

"Hey," said Sheila.

"Has the reading started?" said Elinor.

"Who's reading?" said Sheila, in a very fake-sounding voice.

"There's a lot of people," said Nicole in a distracted way, looking at the top of Sheila's head. "I just saw Richard Cooley."

"Wow," said Elinor. Mike's favorite journalist! Richard Cooley! Elinor involuntarily looked at Sheila to see if she was impressed by this reference. Sheila seemed oblivious.

"I didn't know he had a beard," said Nicole. "He's kind of really hot."

"Where is he?" said Elinor.

"He's over there," said Nicole, pointing to a small man with a very pointy beard who had glasses on.

"Oh, wow," said Elinor.

"Who's he?" said Sheila in her fake-friendly voice again. "I'm sorry, I'm so ignorant. Even though I actually majored in this for like, a year."

"You aren't ignorant," said Nicole, laughing uncomfortably. "He's just this reporter who writes amazing stuff about like, Goldman Sachs. He really hates them. He called them like, a flesh-eating bacteria in an article. It was amazing."

"I don't know who that is," said Sheila. She sighed. "I had the worst day."

"I'm going to tweet about this. I'm going to say I'm weirdly attracted to him. I don't even care if it's weird." Nicole bent her head over her phone and started tweeting.

"So, anyway," said Sheila, in a slightly confidential tone. "I was just so pissed about this shifts thing. It's just disrespectful. You know? Also, I guess I was in a bad mood today. I had my period. Ralph came over last night, and it's like, I don't know, should this guy even be in my life?"

"Ralph's sort of her boyfriend," said Elinor to Gretchen, because Gretchen had come out of the bathroom and was smiling at them like she wanted to be included. Elinor was annoyed that Sheila was talking just loud enough so that Gretchen could hear, but not clearly enough at Gretchen so that she could participate.

"No he's not. He's actually my platonic roommate? We just have a weird relationship." Sheila laughed like a newscaster, and gave Elinor a dirty look. Elinor had forgotten she was like this around strangers.

"Yeah, I've been there," said Gretchen.

"What are we talking about, ladies?" said Nicole, popping her head up from her phone.

"Nothing really," said Sheila.

"No one is liking my tweet or my Instagram?" said Nicole. "But I feel like it's not a good picture. I only got the side of his head. Maybe I'll take it down."

"You take down pictures that don't do well?" said Sheila, incredulously.

"Yeah," said Nicole, defiantly. "You don't?"

"I just figure it's my experience," said Sheila piously. "Obviously, it affects me if I don't get a ton of likes, but I don't really care. My Instagram is literally what I did that day."

No one responded to that.

"Oh, look," said Nicole. "The reading is about to start."

And it was true. There was requisite shuffling, and then Richard Cooley went to the front of the room and took out a sheaf of papers and put them on a lectern.

. . .

The reading lasted a long time, it seemed. Elinor started spacing out during it, looking at the other people, who all seemed in rapt attention. After the reading, she and Sheila took a cab uptown even though Elinor paid for most of it because her commute was so much longer.

"That was fun," said Elinor. "Wasn't it?"

"Yeah," said Sheila. "That's a cool place. I'd never been there before."

"Isn't it? It's a super cool place."

"And I liked your friends. They weren't really into talking though?"

"They are really into their phones, I know," said Elinor.

"I liked them," said Sheila, as she tried to turn off the taxi TV.

"Yeah," said Elinor. "I think they are really interesting."

"I said they were really nice," said Sheila. "Wasn't that the first thing I said?"

"It was," said Elinor, unwilling to take her up on it. Sheila looked at her phone, and Elinor looked at her phone. Mike was green on Facebook chat. She had a perverse desire to say something to him. Why couldn't she? It was so stupid that she couldn't. But what did she even want to say? Maybe the whole problem was that Mike had always secretly thought she was dumb because she didn't write think pieces. Well, fuck him, if that was true! What a dick thing. But then, maybe she was dumb—or at the very least dumber than he was, which was why he needed to leave her. At once, she felt a kind of dissociative anxiety, a pain in her arm. She whispered the word "shit" and opened the window.

"Why did you say 'shit'?" asked Sheila.

"I forgot I had to do something," said Elinor.

. . .

By the time Elinor got back to her apartment, she was tired. She had trouble getting the door open because a rectangular brown box was blocking the vestibule. She could see through the glass door that the box wasn't for her or for Kathy, but for a man named Bob Dole, who lived in a unit called 3A. Did a man named Bob Dole live in their building? She knew there were other tenants, intellectually, because there were other silver mailboxes with other names on them, but she'd never examined the matter closely, or seen these other tenants in the flesh. She wondered if they had shared bathrooms as well.

Elinor finally opened the door and walked up the stairs and into her room. It was messy. She hadn't yet been able to afford one of those stand-up closet things, so she just had her clothing in a suitcase, crumpled in balls. She often missed the apartment she shared with Mike, which even had a bathtub and room for a desk.

Perhaps the reader might be questioning why Elinor was so obsessed with Mike even though he never answered any of her emails and maybe had another girlfriend. Shouldn't she just move on? They didn't even have that good of a relationship! Readers, I don't even know what to tell you. Rapidly, the whole thing had dissolved into boring societal and symbolic forces that went well beyond Mike, but somehow applied to him, like most affairs of the heart.

Elinor sat down on the foam pad and rolled her comforter up over her legs. She propped her computer up on her lap. Without really thinking about it, she opened Word on her computer. All of a sudden, she was seized with the inspiration for a great personal essay and cultural commentary.

She didn't even torture herself and look at Instagram, Facebook, and Twitter all in a row, like she usually did. Instead, she started writing in a torrent.

Recently, I was at a party where almost everyone there was talking about the different pieces they were writing for various publications. All of them were personal essays or opinion essays—and I immediately felt a little intimidated. Although my job working at Journalism.ly makes me cover the news cycle, I don't usually write about myself or my opinions.

At one point, someone suggested I write a piece about a devastating breakup I had recently experienced. I was shocked. I looked around the group of brilliant, interesting women I was with. Did they agree? It seemed as if they did. Some of the women there even insisted that writing about your breakup is a cathartic experience. I left the party mulling over their words. There was a part of me that wanted to give a voice to my experience. But can I really reduce my ex-boyfriend to a think piece?

The truth of it was, my breakup was all I had been thinking about for months. My boyfriend and I (I'll call him "he") had one of those devastatingly adorable meet cutes. He accidentally sat at my table in a coffee shop. I had recognized him from a class we had taken together, and we started talking. We traded witty barbs and trivia about ourselves that was startlingly similar (our rooms growing up were set up in the exact same way, which was just weird, actually). After that moment, we started hanging out constantly, and after several years, eventually living together. I loved the way he snored, the way he argued with the accepted truths of society, and his emotionally intense nature. Sure, sometimes he flinched in the face of intimacy. He would sometimes go dark for days and ignore me when we were out at parties. His moods were changeable and flickering, like the telescope I loved as a child that I never could quite see through. I told myself that that was natural, that we were young, that sometimes I had an intense nature too, and perhaps it overwhelmed him. I was struggling myself, trying to make it as a journalist, and sometimes I took his helpful remarks too personally, feeling like he didn't really respect my writing. Maybe I was moody sometimes, and maybe I overreacted to things, but I thought we were happy. I didn't realize that anything was wrong. I was too in love.

Our breakup, therefore, was unexpected. One day, I returned home and I was greeted with the news that our relationship was over. He was calm. I was not and I'm not proud of it. I screamed. I cried. I begged. He moved out that day. Ever since that day, I've barely heard from him again. I've gone over it and over it in my mind. Why was the breakup of a relationship that meant so much to me so whimpering in its end? In a culture that celebrates lifelong loves and soul mates and being chosen, what do you do when you are rejected and left?

I had to reestablish my identity outside the confines of my relationship, which was both freeing and terrifying. I was free to pursue my ambitions and started developing interests I never had. I started walking everywhere, I moved to a different apartment, and I did things I never thought I would do. At the same time, I missed him. I realized I didn't need to be chosen, I didn't need to be in a relationship to be happy, but I still missed him so much.

One thing I didn't realize is that a breakup means that you completely lose touch with everything about the person. Gone are their T-shirts and their music, but also the friendships and networks you made during that time. I became really good friends with his mom, and luckily I preserved that relationship a little, but it's not the same as it was before. I know in my heart that "he" is a feminist and an ally, it was one of the things I fell in love with him for, but sometimes I wonder, Is it feminist that I have to give up everything and he has to give up nothing? Feminism is about choices, but in this situation I have no choices at all. I have to give up my relationship, and have to have a "take" on what happened, in 500 words? When will he be forced to do that?

There is a part of me that understands why I SHOULD write about my breakup. It is especially important for women to write about themselves because women's narratives have been silenced over the years, just as their labors have been ignored and their feelings shunted aside. Women weren't allowed to tell stories. So I am proud to be of a generation that gives voice to women and helps to mentor and highlight different women writers as they come along.

I know that our time together was complicated, a collage of memories that swirl together to create one chaotic image that sometimes I can't see. I remember vividly a day when we ate pizza and crossed the Brooklyn Bridge, arguing the whole way about whether he was paying enough attention to me on

*social media. All I can do is try to find lessons in that—that
I am more than the worst day of my life. That I am strong.
That I am not defined by my breakup. And that I don't need
to be in a relationship to be happy.*

*So for now, I'm not going to write about my breakup. This
is my choice, and we shouldn't pressure people to do what they
don't want to do. The world needs to respect my choice not to
have a "take" on what happened. They want me to say that
he was an asshole, or I was an asshole. Neither of us was.
It's okay to keep your IRL private life separate from your
professional life and we should totally respect both choices.*

*And if I ever see "him" again, I'll know in my heart that I
was fair, or that it doesn't matter. Because there is no fairness
in love.*

Elinor, satisfied, gave the article a quick proofread and
posted it to the site. She gave it the title "Why Women Need to
Stop Pressuring Each Other to Write About Their Breakups."
Then she fell into a dreamless sleep.

Chapter 10

Facebook: 1 post: "Shameless self-promotion here, but please check out this recent essay I wrote for Journalism.ly about how women shouldn't be pressured to talk about their breakups on social media. I really worked hard on it!" Fifty likes.

Twitter: 2 tweets: "(1/2) Just want to let you guys know I wrote something incredibly personal." "(2/2) Pls be kind but at the same time, know that I am privileged to tell my story and that many people are not, especially in these polarizing times." Four favorites, one retweet, one reply: "So brave!" from a girl from her college class.

Instagram: 1 picture: a quote, white lettering on a black background: "Sometimes a person cannot be beaten or conquered. And that person is beautiful." Eleven likes.

. . .

When Elinor work up that morning, the article was doing decently well. It had gotten three comments and about a hundred shares. One of the comments said, "First"; the other comment said, "Brave piece," and a third comment said, "I understand what you're saying, but the most important thing to remember is that you need to be true to yourself, and love yourself. That is the only way to be happy." Despite the slightly hectoring tone of the last missive, Elinor was pretty pleased. She had gotten comments on the coffee piece and also the tea piece, but they were mostly of the "Coffee's the best" or "I had coffee once and I spilled it on me" variety. The Vans sneakers one got barely any comments because it did so terribly. She never got any personal feedback on her writing. It was a really nice feeling. Elinor decided to post the essay on her various social media profiles too. She hesitated briefly before she did it. Would Mike be offended if he read it? It was hard to say, but probably not. She didn't mention him by name. And at the very least, Mike would know that she was moving on with her life, which was some kind of triumph in some kind of world.

Elinor trudged down the hall with her makeup kit and her small makeup mirror and her brush and her hair dryer and her change of clothing under her arm. The bathroom itself consisted of gray subway tile with an old claw-foot tub and a showerhead that spurted water like a semiautomatic weapon.

Elinor got out of the shower and blew dry her hair and did her makeup carefully, even putting eye shadow on. She felt much better today. The depression of yesterday had lifted somewhat.

Elinor walked back to her room. She put her wet towel in what was acting as her hamper (a small plastic bag from Gristedes that was sitting on the floor, rather forlornly stuffed with socks and underwear), and pulled on a tentlike garment she had recently purchased. Then she checked her phone. Her essay had six comments, which was pretty usual for a piece on Journalism.ly, a website that in general did not have very active commenters. And they were three more nice things! Maybe this would be another viral piece, although the shares weren't that high. She put her phone in her bag, put her coat on, and walked down to the subway.

. . .

Elinor had experienced virality before. "15 Things Only Coffee Lovers Know" and the murdering psychopath quiz had both gone viral, and she had felt the pleasant glow of people liking things that she had done and recognizing themselves in her work. But she had never yet gotten virality based on the back of her actual long-form writing. So she was a bit unprepared when streams of comments and tweets and Instagram likes decided to weigh in on what she had said. Elinor monitored all of this with an avid precision. Some were flattering—"I really super get what this writer is going through. I had a boyfriend who sucked, but what I realized is that this author needs to love herself. Learning to love yourself is the world's greatest gift." Then there were some meaner comments. "It's clear that this author knows nothing about life. Boo hoo, her boyfriend left her. She needs to get a life. Go out and volunteer or something. Step outside your bubble." Or "Why is she saying she DIDN'T write a take on this guy. She's clearly so obsessed with him, it's weird." Then there was simply a comment from someone called dylansdad_57_289, who just said, "Go die you whore."

By the time she got to work, Elinor's piece had gotten a hundred comments. This was unheard of at Journalism.ly. Every single time Elinor refreshed her page there was another comment. Peter approached her almost the minute she came in the door. She was just hanging her coat up on a much-abused rack.

"You posted an essay last night," said Peter.

"Yeah," said Elinor.

"It got a lot of comments."

"I know."

"That's good. Don't worry if there are mean comments."

"Are there more mean comments? I mean, I didn't like 'Go die you whore,' but I read that you can't really do anything about stuff like that. I guess I could write an essay about my reaction to that comment? That would be kind of interesting—"

"I'm not saying there are more mean comments now. I don't know if there will be. Maybe there won't be. All I'm saying is not to let it get to you."

"Okay," said Elinor. "Do you think everyone is going to be really mean?"

"No," said Peter. "But the essay is pretty personal, so . . ."

"Well, it's actually about how women need to take ownership of their stories. I'm actually talking about how there is pressure on me to write a personal essay. It's not what you are saying at all."

"You are very very defensive. And I say that as a mentor," said Peter.

"I'm just stressed."

"It's fine. Forget it." Peter walked back to his desk and Elinor walked to hers. Nicole was already sitting down. She didn't look up when Elinor pulled the chair out next to her.

"Hey!" said Elinor. She tapped Nicole on the shoulder. At this prompting, Nicole took off her headphones.

"Oh, hi," said Nicole.

"I had such a fun time last night. Thanks for inviting me."

"No problem."

"I really liked your friends. They are such cool girls."

"Yeah, they are fun." Nicole wasn't looking at her. She was looking at her computer.

"Yeah, it was so fun." Elinor sighed. "I actually wrote a piece when I got home, about what we were talking about."

"I saw!"

"Yeah," said Elinor, suddenly wondering (too late) if Nicole would think she was talking about her and her friends in the essay she wrote. But she wasn't even talking about them! It was more about like, the principle of the thing. "It wasn't really about last night. I more used the friend thing as like, a metaphor."

"Oh I know," said Nicole.

"Okay, phew," said Elinor. Nicole put her headphones on, and Elinor put her headphones on. That was a relief! Nicole wasn't mad, even though she didn't say anything that nice about Elinor's article, which was kind of mean.

The rest of the day, Elinor was distracted by the constant interactions that were happening on her article. Despite the fact that it technically saw far fewer "views" perhaps than "15 Things Only Coffee Lovers Know," it seemed far more discussed, which made Elinor feel far more like an "influencer" than anything else had previously. Every so often a new comment would bubble up, incendiary or complimentary, and after a while Elinor couldn't even keep track of them anymore or want to cry when she saw them. At the end of the day, it seemed to her, it had been the most talked-about story on the Internet.

By the end of the second day, it had even inspired responses in other places. There was one that was called "Why I Will Write About My Breakup No Matter What," and it was on a fashion blog Elinor had never read. It explicitly mentioned Elinor's article!

Around noontime, she even got an email with the subject line "TV APPEARANCE."

Elinor's hand shook when she clicked on it.

Hello, this is Keisha O'Donnell at New York 1. We loved your article at the 5 o'clock news and we'd love to have you on! You will be in conversation with a professor, Kevin Lang, who wrote a book called *The Surveillance State and Online Dating.* We won't be doing hair and makeup.

Elinor wrote back, her hands cramping from excitement, "I just need to inform my boss, but that sounds great!"

She got up so quickly her chair made a scraping sound.

. . .

When she went up to J.W. in his glass conference room to inform him of her TV opportunity, he seemed a bit dazed.

"You're doing what?" he said. Elinor was right. J.W. was dazed. He had been daydreaming about what kinds of calamities would occur if he lost his job again. He was oftentimes worried about the fate of the Journalism.ly. On some fundamental level, he had never understood the company's fortunes.

For example, the Journalism.ly had recently suffered a spate of unexplained disappearances and firings. In the plus column, this meant that many of J.W.'s young, bespectacled adversaries were slowly being dispatched. The receptionist, who always rolled his eyes at J.W., got fired some months ago for stealing money and they never replaced him. A guy named Tim had left on his own accord to do something with bicycle riding? And they never replaced him. Yet on the negative side of things, what if this thinning of the staff meant that the Journalism.ly was about to collapse and J.W. was going to get fired too? Sean always said they had no money. Sometimes he would seem worried about it—at which point, he would make some sort of speech about going viral more. But sometimes Sean would buy gigantic yoga balls for everyone to sit on instead of chairs, so maybe they did have money? It was all extremely confusing.

"I'm going on television! They want me to be on television! New York One."

"Okay," said J.W. This was good news. Who could ever fire a man, nay a reporter, who'd hired someone who went on New York 1? They simply couldn't. "We should probably tell Sean?"

"Okay!" said Elinor. Then she laughed way too loud, which was embarrassing.

They walked the short, yet needlessly confusing route to Sean's office. They had to leave the Journalism.ly and cross through the reception area where Yellow Suspenders never even sat anymore. Elinor didn't know what had happened to him. One day, he had simply vanished.

When they got to the office, Sean and Katya were inside. You could see them through the glass walls that separated his office from the reception area. Sean was on the phone, and Katya, looking particularly ill, made a gesture that told them to wait in the small anteroom where they were congregating. Elinor and J.W. looked at each other, and Elinor realized she had never really spent time with J.W. in an unstructured setting.

"So," said Elinor, hitting her shoe against the back of her leg, accidentally. For a moment she lost her balance. "Have you been busy?"

"Yes," said J.W., giving Sean's office a desperate look. "So so busy."

"Where do you live?"

"We might move," said J.W. "It's hard to drive back and forth from where we are. But we might stay. I don't know. Don't tell Sean we're thinking of moving."

"I'm not going to!" said Elinor.

Katya came out of the office. She was wearing high-heeled shoes. She was the only person in the office, in fact, who ever wore high-heeled shoes or skirts. Sometimes, Elinor wondered if she felt lonely, as if she were working in a far better office somewhere else but no one knew.

"Sean just needs one more minute. He's doing a call."

J.W. and Elinor waited in the anteroom for ten more minutes in silence. Elinor looked at her phone and J.W. looked at his phone.

Just when their silence was starting to become provocative, Katya returned and ushered them into the office. Sean was sitting with his feet up on his desk, which was actually a very large, midcentury modern table with a portrait-size Apple computer on it. He gestured to two Eames chairs in front of the desk. J.W. and Elinor sat down in them. J.W. took the one slightly closer to Sean.

"Well, what can I do for you guys?" Sean smiled at them.

"We had a big piece of success," said J.W. "One of our pieces went viral and we were offered a chance on the five p.m. news."

"That's great," said Sean. "About the election? Josh's piece on election shaming? Do they want me to go on?"

"They contacted me!" said Elinor, a bit too loudly.

"It's a personal essay," said J.W. apologetically. "About dating."

"Do you have any experience on television?" said Sean. "You're fine to do it. But I think it's important to have a bit of media training."

"I took a course in college," said Elinor. "But I mean, obviously you can go on in my place. I mean, I'm sure you would be much better than me."

"No, no," said Sean. "You should go on. It's your piece. Just be sure to mention the fact that the story came from the Journalism.ly, okay? Good job! No, really."

"Oh I don't know." Elinor was pleased.

"Take pride in it! That's a great thing! Women shouldn't just be humble. They need to take pride in their accomplishments. Take pride in it!"

"Okay," said Elinor.

"Is that all?" said Sean. "Great work, J.W. and Elinor."

"Thanks," said J.W., standing up. Elinor also stood up. The meeting was over. Elinor exited quickly, but J.W. lingered, his eyes hovering along the ceiling. Perhaps he needed further, increasingly pointed congratulation. In any case, he didn't say anything, and touched a paperweight on Sean's desk with one finger.

"Good job on getting her on TV, J.W.," said Sean, faithfully taking up his cue.

"Thanks."

"She was a recommendation from Pam Johnson, right? Speaking of which, are you going to her Memorial Day party?"

"Uh, no?" said J.W.

"Come with me," said Sean. "I'd love for you to talk about our branded content gaming strategy with Mike Soloman from the *Times*. I think he's going to be there."

"Uh, yes, absolutely," said J.W. He smiled at Sean, but inside he felt a sense of dread. He hadn't been to a journalism party in four years. In his previous life, he used to be able to say that he was a columnist who wrote "Thoughts and Musings." It wasn't Pam Johnson level, but it was something. And now, he was going to have to say that he essentially did nothing. All the feelings of failure he had tried to smother in a haze of grateful-ness for a living wage came flooding back.

"Good!" said Sean. That was J.W.'s cue to leave.

. . .

Halfway through her hair appointment at a butter-yellow hair salon that just did blow-dries, Elinor realized she had noth-ing to wear on TV. While her hair was being pulled taut by a round brush, she texted Sheila about borrowing her black dress. Sheila, who happened to be home, told Elinor to pick the dress up at her apartment. And so, right after the appoint-ment was over, she walked the twenty blocks to Sheila's.

Sheila answered the door in their college's sweatshirt.

"Hey!" she said. "How was the TV thing?"

"It hasn't happened yet," said Elinor. "That's why I'm getting the dress from you. Fuck! I'm so nervous."

"I'm sure you are going to do a great job," said Sheila, in an absentminded way. "I have leftover pizza in the oven. Do you want any of it?"

"Maybe like, one slice? But I don't know. I have that TV thing, and I don't want to look fat. Where are your roommates?" All five of them seemed to have vacated the premises. This almost never happened at Sheila's. The roommates were always around, whispering.

"Actually all of them are out. Three are at work and we still haven't filled the room that Ralph was going to be in. We have to start like, putting an ad on Craigslist or something. Do you think we will get someone weird?"

"What happened with Ralph?" said Elinor. "Are you serious?"

"Fuck, I mean. He's a dick. I don't know. I don't know why I trusted him to not be a dick."

"What happened? Why didn't you tell me?" said Elinor. "Also, where is the dress?"

"I put it on the couch."

Elinor walked over to the couch and saw the dress lying limply over the back of it. She took the dress in her hands and held it up to her. She had tried it on before. She always thought it looked better on her than it looked on Sheila. She wished Sheila would just give it to her. She would have given it to Sheila if the situation was reversed.

"Basically he told me he was going to move in here, which I told you like, a while ago?"

"Yes," said Elinor. Perhaps she said this in a slightly bitter tone. If so, it wasn't like she meant to do it. In any case, Sheila gave her a barely perceptible look.

"And we were talking every single night and it never ever seemed like he was changing his mind or anything. And then like, a week ago, we spent all night hanging out, and we slept in the same bed but we didn't hook up."

"Sheila," said Elinor. "I don't even believe that."

"We didn't!" said Sheila. "And then after that, after we had an amazing night together where we just like, talked about our lives. Then the next day he texts me, and he's like, 'I'm not going to move in.' And I'm like, shocked, okay? Because we had been talking and talking and talking about it and then he just basically pulled out when we had almost no time to find anyone else?"

"Why did he say he was not going to move in with you?"

"That he thinks it will be too awkward? That like, we have too much 'weirdness' between us?"

"Well," said Elinor. "Maybe this isn't the worst thing that could happen."

"I mean, I know. You're right. Maybe it wasn't the smartest idea anyway."

Elinor was feeling slightly beatific from her brush with fame. She gave Sheila a knowing smile.

"Yeah, I don't know," said Elinor. "I don't think I would have done it. You know, it's not very feminist to put yourself in this position."

"How so?" said Sheila, Elinor noticed, with a slightly dangerous uptick to her voice.

"Well, did you read my article?"

"Yeah, sure."

"I was kind of talking about this. You can't just like, let these things happen to you, you know? That's not feminist. If you had known that he wasn't treating you right, I think you should have told him like, all of this wasn't acceptable."

"I know," said Sheila. "I mean, I know I was dumb. That doesn't help me."

"I guess," said Elinor, "it's not that you were dumb, it's more that you weren't thinking of it at all in context, you know?"

Sheila glowered at her.

"All I'm going to say," said Sheila, "is that you totally would have done it with Mike. Move in with him and stuff. Like, if he called you now? You would totally move in with him."

"No. I don't think I would have at all," said Elinor. "Mike and I had a very mature breakup. Neither of us were assholes."

"You totally wanted to get back with him. You are still going to the fucking party his mother is having!"

"I am going to the party his mother is having because we are trying to be friends and she has been an amazing professional contact. That's why I am going."

"Uh, okay."

"Listen," said Elinor, in her newfound patient voice. "I know you are hurting about Ralph but don't take it out on me. Anyway, I have to go on TV in like, two seconds—"

"I'm not taking it out on you," said Sheila. "I just hate that you always act like you would never do the things that I would do or something. When you totally would have! You are so condescending sometimes."

"Condescending! What the fuck are you talking about? I'm not condescending to you!"

"Yes you fucking are. You think you are so much better than me. And you're totally fucking not, is the thing. It's all fake too. I mean, you wrote that whole post to get Mike back or to get back at him. Either-or. Whatever it was, it was the exact same thing as what I did."

"Sheila," said Elinor. She was, all of a sudden, quite angry. "Are you kidding me? What you don't understand is that that was feminist! I was being a feminist and you are like, the least feminist person in the world."

"See?" said Sheila. "This is exactly what I'm talking about. This is the condescending way that you talk to me, like you are so amazing just because you are a journalist and are going on TV. You talk to me like you are trying to explain feminism to me. It's really pathetic."

"Oh, fuck off, Sheila, seriously. You are just jealous of me. I can't believe that you are actually jealous that I have a good life now! Which is sick!"

"I'm not jealous of that," said Sheila. "I'm not jealous of you. I just hate the way you treat me like I'm stupid or lame. I'm neither. You are the exact same as me. If you think I'm pathetic, then you are pathetic too."

"Fuck you! You just always fuck up your life and now you want to blame me," said Elinor. She grabbed the dress and left to go on TV.

. . .

Elinor was still fuming from her fight with Sheila when she changed into her dress in a Starbucks bathroom. However, when she finally arrived at the sliding glass doors of the TV building, her nerves took over. She waited on an oblong leather couch in the lobby for someone to pick her up, which was what she had been instructed to do.

After ten minutes or so, a publicist came into the lobby. She was carrying a clipboard and a gigantic walkie-talkie. She gave Elinor a very firm handshake.

"Sorry we're late! We've been super stressed up there," she said. "I'm Erin."

"Oh, no worries at all! I'm just excited to be going on TV, I actually really am."

"Well, that's great. We're really happy to have you too."

Elinor followed Erin through a very cold, nondescript hall and into a large steel elevator to the tenth floor, where they got out and walked down more hallways that were lined with black-and-white pictures of great events, like Kennedy visiting New York in a gigantic white car. At the end of this hallway, there was a small closet flooded with light. This was the room where Elinor was going to wait. It had a mirror surrounded by circular lightbulbs, like some matinee idol's bathroom. It also had a bunch of makeup spilling out of a huge black toolbox.

"So this is the makeup room. Just chill in here in case I call you. Okay?"

"Okay," said Elinor. "Can I have a glass of water?"

"Of course," said Erin. Elinor sat down on a director's chair directly facing the mirror. Erin rushed out of the room carrying her clipboard.

Elinor looked at herself in the mirror. She had bags under her eyes the shape of wet tea bags. She was extremely thirsty, and yet she also had to pee. But where was the bathroom? Elinor didn't think it was appropriate for her to start wandering.

Eventually, Erin came back with the water. Elinor drank it greedily.

"We'll call for you in like, five to ten minutes, okay?"

"Okay," said Elinor in a thick gulp. "Can you also announce me as Elinor Tomlinson, from the Journalism.ly? It's how my boss wants you to announce me."

"Sure," said Erin brusquely. She left the room.

Thirty minutes passed. Elinor looked at her phone. She Instagrammed a picture of the makeup room (she hoped Sheila saw it and felt bad because she was such a huge bitch), she finished her water and had to pee even more than before. She refreshed her makeup with her own makeup, which she had brought in her bag.

Ten minutes after that, Erin came back. She was a little breathless and still holding a clipboard, but now she had a headset on.

"Okay, so, unfortunately we're kind of running behind on time today, can you believe it?"

"Oh no!" said Elinor.

"Yes, which is, you know, kind of stressful—so your segment is going to be a bit shorter than we thought it was going to be. Which should be fine for you? We're going to bring in a sociologist to talk about the Internet and dating more generally before you get on there, and then you will say a little something. Okay?"

"Um, wait, am I going to be going on at a different time?"

"I wish I could explain," said Erin. She was outwardly making some semblance of a sympathetic expression, but Elinor could see she was actually annoyed. "But we really have to go. You might miss your slot or something. Follow me?"

"Do you know where the bathroom is?"

"Do you mind waiting until after the segment?" said Erin.

"No!" said Elinor. "Not at all."

They walked out of the makeup room and down another long hall. Elinor passed a bathroom. Then the stage appeared before her. At first, all she could see was a long, dark cavern. Maybe a hundred feet away, she spotted two news anchors who were looking at papers on their desk and not talking to each other. A picture of the New York City skyline was behind them. There was a single cameraman, who was holding a large camera attached to a dolly with a cord.

"Okay," said Erin. "We have to whisper in here. They are just about to shoot and like, you can't really talk. I'll cue you when you need to take your seat. Okay?"

"Okay," said Elinor in a barely audible whisper. She looked around her. Ten feet away was a solitary chair. Erin started to walk toward the cameraman and whisper in his ear, and then Elinor moved to the chair, because she was too nervous to stand.

"And we're back. And we're here to talk about dating and the Internet!" said a news anchor. "There's Tinder. There's OkCupid. But is there Yelp for dating? And should there be?"

The camera paused for a brief second on the news anchor's face before turning toward another screen, where a montage of images flickered on the screen (the Tinder logo, the OkCupid logo, and then some people walking around New York City). Elinor couldn't hear what was being said (it was prerecorded and obviously playing off camera). During this entire montage, the newscasters just looked at their papers again.

They did not seem to have a particularly cordial relationship offscreen.

Suddenly Elinor became aware of another shape in the dark next to her, accompanied by Erin. This shape seemed to resemble an older male, who looked a bit scholarly, but in what Elinor thought was a handsome way. He had thick black glasses on. He looked like a Brooklyn dad. The Brooklyn dad waved to Elinor and hissed, "Hi!" Elinor waved back.

"Okay," said Erin to the dad, not acknowledging Elinor. "It's time for you to go on."

The dad simply nodded and followed Erin up to the table, where there was now an empty seat waiting for him. When did they set that up? Elinor saw that there was another empty chair up there, for her.

Erin raced back to Elinor. She was holding a giant Walkman attached to several wires.

"Here," she said, shoving it at Elinor. Elinor held the device, not knowing quite what to do with it.

"Attach the mike part to the top of your dress? I'll fasten the speaker to your back," she said.

Elinor mutely attached what looked like a tiny microphone to the top of her collar. Erin went around to her back and got busy clipping the back of the mike to the top of her pocket. The mike was very very cold. Elinor watched the Brooklyn dad's interview.

"Good to have you with us, Professor."

"It's good to be here," said the Brooklyn dad.

"Do you think the Internet is good for the dating culture?" said the male interviewer.

"It has changed it," said the Brooklyn dad. In the light, Elinor noticed that the Brooklyn dad had beautiful gray, curly hair that wasn't receding at all. "Now everything is available on the Internet all the time."

"How so?" said the female newscaster.

"Millennials can really research their dates in an unprecedented way. They can Google practically everything about their prospective partners. But does that lead to better relationships?"

"We'll be right back with more after the break," said the male newscaster.

"Okay, you need to go up now," said Erin. "Go up there."

Elinor traversed the very dark stage to the elevated news desk, at which the male newscaster, the female newscaster, and the Brooklyn dad were sitting. She sat down in the empty seat next to the Brooklyn dad. The female newscaster was making small talk with him.

"So how did you become an expert in modern dating?" said the female newscaster. She was making a lot of eye contact with the Brooklyn dad.

"Well, I'm a sociologist and my work just naturally led me there."

"That's amazing," said the female newscaster.

"We're back in three, two, one," said the cameraman.

"And we're back," said the female newscaster, "and we're here with Kevin Lang, professor of sociology at CUNY Brooklyn, and Elinor Tomlinson, a blogger at the Journalism.ly, which is a news website on the Internet. And we're talking about dating. Elinor, you recently wrote a blog about how women shouldn't tell their dating stories? Why was that?"

"Uh, yes!" said Elinor. "Although it wasn't really about that. It was more about how you are encouraged to write about all this stuff with your dating life, and you know, maybe things just didn't work out and you, um, you know, it's just confusing, and, um, women shouldn't feel pressure to write about their breakups if they don't want to."

"But what's great about the Internet is everyone's unique voice," said the Brooklyn dad. "I think the idea that you can't tell your story is historically bad for women. You are selling them short."

"I wasn't really trying to sell anyone short really?" said Elinor. Her throat was hot. "That's not what I was doing. I actually said in the essay that historically women were stopped from telling stories on a structural level."

"The Internet is democratic?" said the female newscaster.

"Exactly!" said the Brooklyn dad. "And women should be able to talk about whatever they want."

"Sure, I wasn't even saying like—" said Elinor.

"I think it's fantastic that people are free to choose how to express themselves."

"Oh, me too," said Elinor, worried that a flush was suffusing her entire face. "Like, of course I think that too."

During all this, the male newscaster was visibly not paying attention. He must not have been on-screen. Now, however, he sprang back into action.

"Thank you so much, Kevin and Elinor," he said. "Next, this panda thinks he's a dog!"

A brief but jaunty music played.

"Well, thanks, guys," said the female newscaster. "I appreciate you both coming out here."

"It was my pleasure," said the Brooklyn dad. He had a wedding ring on, Elinor realized.

Erin appeared out of the morass of the darkness.

"Guys, that was great," she said. The Brooklyn dad was already getting up. Elinor followed him.

"When do you think I can tweet the link to my appearance?" said Elinor to Erin.

"It should be up later on tonight," said Erin.

"Thanks," said Elinor. She had been on TV! She would worry about it later.

. . .

Outside the studio Elinor sat on the curb.

She took her phone out and looked at it. Some texts and tweets had surfaced since she had written the words "Can't wait to be on TV" but fewer than she would have expected, honestly. And nothing from Sheila, who had completely attacked her for no reason. Bitch.

It was then she got a text from Will, the crossword puzzle guy. She hadn't heard from him in weeks.

"Did I just see you on New York 1? Don't usually watch the news."

Despite how shook she was, Elinor decided to write back quickly.

"Yes! How are you?"

There was no response.

Chapter 11

Facebook: 2 posts. Post 1: "For anyone who was offended by my TV appearance about women writing about their breakups, I'm so sorry. Obviously anyone should be able to write about whatever they want to, they just shouldn't feel pressure. That was the real point." Three likes, no comments.

Post 2: "Hey guys. I just want to say thanks! Thanks for being there for me in these past couple of months. Thanks for letting me be me. Thanks for letting me know how much you care. I really appreciate it, especially in these polarizing times. I wouldn't have had such success without all the support I've been given. #Grateful #thankyou #blessed."

Instagram: 1 picture: Of a group of girls (Elinor is included) at a dark, small restaurant in Brooklyn filled with tiny wooden tables. The filter is slightly yellow, and most people (including Elinor) are wearing smocks. Caption: "#ballers."

Snapchat: A short video of Elinor in the makeup room at New York 1, with a filter that turns her eyes into mouths!

So tell me about yourself," said Devin. That was the guy's name—Devin. Elinor had met him on a site called Coffee Meets Bagel. In his picture, his hair had been carefully slicked to the side in a small bouffant, and he had been leaning toward someone who was cut out of the photo.

"Um, what can I say? I don't know, that's such a weird question, I guess," said Elinor. She was tired. Peter had told her she needed to redo a list she wrote called "10 Reasons Why Vans Sneakers Are Pretty Punk Rock." He wanted to delete three of the reasons, but he didn't say which ones.

"How is it a weird question?" asked Devin.

"It's not, I'm sorry," said Elinor. "It's just such a New York dating question. You know?"

"I just moved here," said Devin.

"Oh. Well, you'll see," said Elinor mysteriously.

"Okay." Devin looked confused.

"It's just—no one ever says anything different. Everyone is like, the same person. It's really exhausting."

"How can everyone be the same person?"

"No, whatever, it's fine," said Elinor. "I've just been on so many dates at this point. The apps are so bad."

"Which ones have you done?" Devin was wearing a very tight blue sweater and his eyes were much closer together than they looked in photos. In fact, they were closer together than she had ever seen eyes be. "I've only done Coffee Meets Bagel."

. . .

The next weeks were sad ones for Elinor. She didn't really talk to Sheila, which actually gave her a lot of free time, as Sheila constantly chatted her while she was at work. She was therefore productive, if a little depressed. There were parts of their dispute that would resurface unbidden, usually as she was sitting alone in transportation. Was she really condescending? Had she been a lunatic with Mike? Was it really pathetic to go to the Memorial Day party? But no! It definitely wasn't. It was totally the polite thing to do. They had a relationship because Mike's mother had gotten her a job, et cetera, et cetera, and forever and ever amen.

Her life had assumed a monotonous routine. She lay in Queens on a foam pad most days after work. Nicole still wasn't really talking to her, but Elinor assumed it was because she was doing acupuncture for her anxiety disorder.

Soon, however, it was time for the Memorial Day party. The day it was to occur Elinor paced around her apartment, modeling different outfits, even wearing a scarf at one point (she took it off). One thing that was causing her some perturbation was that she hadn't actually ever seen Mike since Botanica—and he hadn't ever texted. At some point, after her essay, she had assumed she would have heard from him. All he really had to say was "good job" or something, just like she had said about his Iran piece, which she didn't even read. But he stayed silent. Did he not see it? Maybe he saw it and hated it, which would have been crazy. The essay was simply an elegiac paean to the end of a relationship. No one could have possibly been upset by it.

Elinor arrived at the door to Mike's parents' apartment

about twenty minutes after the party had started. This was on purpose. She didn't want to arrive before a critical mass had gathered. She grasped the wine bottle she was carrying, her knuckles a greenish white, and rang the doorbell.

Mike's father answered the door. He was holding a wine bottle, just like Elinor. It was then that she realized she had never spoken to him before.

"Hi, Eben," said Elinor.

"Hello," said Eben. He stepped backward two inches, as if startled.

"I brought some wine."

"We have a lot of wine here already. But thank you."

"I don't really know wine but I talked to the guy at the wine store and he recommended this. I hope it's good? It was sort of expensive."

"I'm sure it's fine. Well, come in!" said Eben. He made a hand motion, and Elinor followed him down a hall that was decorated with black-and-white pictures of Mike and his sister in their youth, wearing matching cable-knit sweaters and standing on a dock.

Elinor had imagined this party many times before she attended it, and thus she had a peculiar sense of déjà vu when she walked into the living room, trailing after Mike's father, and observed the scene. The first thing she noticed was that there were almost no guests present. Two men were sitting on the couch. A group of three was standing next to the window. There was a bunch of open wine bottles, all reds, littered on the mahogany sideboard. Elinor, at a loss for what to do, wandered toward the wine bottles. Mike's father had already darted somewhere else. Mike was nowhere to be found.

At that point, however, she saw Mike's mother. She was balancing a silver tray on one hand and holding the kitchen door open with her foot. Elinor put her wine bottle down next to the other bottles and walked toward her.

"Hi, Pam!" said Elinor. "Can I help you? It's so nice of you to invite me to this party."

"Oh, that's okay." Pam smiled, but her eyes were somehow wider than normal, and Elinor had a fleeting, dreadful thought that Mike's mother didn't know she was coming. But how could that be? She had been invited! Pam shifted the tray to her other hand. "You know Mike's not here yet?"

"Is he coming?" said Elinor.

"He's coming eventually. You know Mike. When has that kid ever been on time?"

"I know!" said Elinor enthusiastically, pleased that Mike's mother was recalling her prior claims. "I mean, I totally do know. He's never on time, ever."

"Well, good to see you—"

"Also, um, I just wanted to thank you again for getting me that job."

"Oh yeah, right. At Journalism.ly." Mike's mother shifted the tray again. It looked quite heavy. There were several different cheeses on it and some pale green, hard-looking grapes.

"Let me help you, please," said Elinor, motioning toward the tray.

"No, that's fine. I should probably put this down over there, so—"

"I just want to say that like, you have really inspired me, as like, an author. I'm writing a lot now."

"That's great."

"I actually just wrote a piece that was kind of about the process in which we write. Just kind of about how we deal with loss and endings. I'd love to get your feedback on it—"

"Ahh," said Mike's mother. It was hard to tell from her face if she knew what Elinor was talking about. It had an inscrutable expression on it. "How interesting. Well, I really have to put this tray down. But thanks for coming."

"Thanks for having me," said Elinor too loud. Her volume control always suffered terribly under stress.

. . .

In an Uber across town, another horror was happening.

In the past week, J.W. had come to the conclusion that he could not attend the Memorial Day party without some reinstatement of "Thoughts and Musings." All the journalists of his generation would be there, still writing their various columns. And when they asked him what he did with his time, he would have to say, what? That he wasn't even writing anymore? That, instead, he was calling up the CEO of Walmart and asking him to write a blog about why unions are bad? It was too much! He had to say something.

It was hard to predict how Sean would take an actual demand from J.W. After his unemployment, J.W. had been far too scared to make demands, and staying quiet seemed to be working really well. No one bothered him, and he had completely commandeered the conference room. People didn't even try to have conferences at all anymore, especially since he put up blinds. Should he really say anything when things were going so well? The entire week J.W. had pondered the subject without incident. On the day of the party, he finally determined he would broach it with Sean while they drove to the party together.

Thus, when the Uber—a shiny black monstrosity with chrome finishes and three sets of seats—arrived at J.W.'s apartment, J.W. was discomfited at the sight of Peter in the second seat next to Sean. J.W. had to step over him on his way back to the third seat.

"Hi, J.W.," said Peter, without moving his legs, which were in the center aisle.

"Hi," said J.W. "Hi, Sean. I didn't know Peter was going to this?"

"I asked Sean what he was doing this weekend, and he told me to come along!" said Peter.

"It's always good to network," said Sean.

"Of course," said J.W. stiffly. He sat down in the third seat and leaned forward, so his face was almost in the second seat.

"I was just telling Sean about this new initiative I was thinking of starting," said Peter. He was leaning against the window, his seat belt unfastened. "I would *love* to get some virtual reality gaming on the site."

"What?" said J.W.

"I'm just trying to think outside the box here. But what if we combined gaming with the news?"

"How would we do that?" said J.W. neutrally.

"Okay, I was playing Pokémon Go, and I just thought, What if we could apply it to news gathering? I know it's outside the box? But that's what we do at the Journalism.ly. We try shit and we see what works."

"Would the Pokémon be stories?" said J.W.

"There isn't any Pokémon in the game. It's the news that would be the game. We would bring gaming to the news."

"I love that idea," said Sean, loudly. "Peter, I love that. J.W., let's make that happen. You be in charge of that. Work with Peter."

"Great," said J.W. He sat back on his seat.

"Did everyone have a good weekend so far?" said Peter.

"I was just thinking!" J.W. yelled. He threw his face forward again "I want to restart 'Thoughts and Musings' at the Journalism.ly."

"What's that? Sure," said Sean.

"I was surprised you didn't continue it when you got here." Peter crossed his arms, as if this truth should have been self-evident. "All of journalism is just opinion now. You were like, the only person not saying their opinion on the entire site."

"Maybe your column could be our first virtual reality gaming column," said Sean, helpfully.

"Yeah," said J.W. "Okay, I'll write the first one next week."

He sat back again. He couldn't tell if he was satisfied or not. On the one hand, he'd gotten what he wanted. On the other, it posed a philosophical question too complicated for J.W. to answer at the moment: Is it foolish to agonize about something that is apparently not a big deal? Still, the only time he was ever happy historically was when he was writing down his own opinions, and this consideration needed to be weighed beyond all others. Plus it was a great thing to say at a party. On the whole, when he fully considered it, he was satisfied.

. . .

Mike still wasn't at the party.

At first, Elinor didn't care. She just texted on her phone, which was what she usually did when she was at a party alone. But soon it became a little awkward, especially as more people showed up. She was the only person texting. Everyone else was talking. She would have talked to Mike's mother more, but she kept running back and forth to the kitchen.

After about ten minutes of texting, Elinor decided to approach a woman wearing red glasses, someone she had seen at Mike's mother's last dinner party. This was an object of some social difficulty, because Red Glasses was talking to a corpulent fellow in an oxford shirt made out of a translucent cotton, and they seemed very absorbed by their conversation. Elinor decided that forthright assurance and commonplace goodwill was the best tack.

"He's not going to win, thank god," the woman in the red glasses was saying, as Elinor approached. "So I'm not worried."

"Hi," said Elinor. "We've met before I think?"

"Yes?" said Red Glasses.

"I went to a dinner party here with you. My name is Elinor?"

"Yes!" said the woman. "Are you here with Mike?"

"Well, Mike's actually not here yet." Elinor let out a flat laugh. "I'm wondering when he's going to arrive."

"This is Bruce by the way."

"Hi, Bruce," said Elinor to the corpulent man, who was also very bald. Bruce nodded.

"So what have you been doing since our dinner party?" Red Glasses pivoted, helpfully, in the direction of Bruce. "Pam had a dinner party about six-ish months ago where I apparently

met Elinor. I'm so sorry. I just don't remember anything anymore. It's my election stress."

"Yeah! Six months ago. What have I been doing?" said Elinor. "I've actually been having a crazy couple of months, but
they have been really great and busy. I got a new job at the
Journalism.ly."

"Sean Patterson's website?" said Bruce, speaking for the first
time. He had an authoritative voice, like the prosecutor in the
Scopes monkey trial.

"Yeah, it's been amazing," said Elinor. "And recently I've
gotten way more into writing long-form pieces, which has been
super great for me. I wrote a really interesting longer thing
recently about the pressure on women to write about their
breakups."

"Why breakups?" said Bruce.

"Well, I just went through a breakup," said Elinor. "I actually had been dating Mike? You know? Pam Johnson's son? We'd
been dating for a while, like, four years? But then we broke up
recently. And it's fine! We're still friends." Elinor saw Mike's
mother walk back into the living room. She was carrying a tray
of phyllo-wrapped canapés that looked like miniature paper
bags. She put them on the sideboard.

"Interesting," said Bruce. "I've never heard that before."

"What?"

"That women are being pressured to write about their
breakups."

"Well, they are," said Elinor sharply. "Like, every day I read
something about a breakup."

"Interesting," said Bruce.

"I went on TV about it, actually."

"That's great," said Red Glasses. "Are you seeing anyone right now?"

Elinor smiled at her, to buy time to recover. She had felt so insulted by Bruce's mild skepticism that she had almost cried, which made her realize that she had been very close to crying the entire time she had been at the party.

"Well, recently I've been dating a lot."

"Yes?" Red Glasses was interested. "Do you use the apps?"

"I do!"

"How are they?"

"I have a friend who is on those apps," said Bruce. "He's divorced."

"I couldn't do it," said Red Glasses. "I don't know how these kids do it. So what is it? Someone messages you?"

"Yeah, and I've gotten some horrible ones. I'll show you."

Elinor took out her phone and started scrolling through her messages. She wondered if this was a good idea but then decided it was.

"Look at this one!" She shoved her phone in the direction of Red Glasses and Bruce.

" 'Hey girl, lol'?" said Bruce. "That's a shitty pickup line. In our day, at a bar, you had to at least talk to someone."

"I know," said Red Glasses. "I really couldn't do this. This is so hard."

"Elinor," said Peter, quietly. He had come up by her shoulder. She had not seen him come in, she didn't know he was coming, his hair was slicked totally down like a helmet, his ears stuck out. It was a shock. "What are you showing these people?"

"Ahh," yelled Elinor. "Peter, you scared me!"

"Hi," said Peter, holding his hand out to Red Glasses and Bruce. "I'm Peter. I work with Elinor at the Journalism.ly."

"Hello," said Red Glasses.

"J.W. and Sean are here too," said Peter, perhaps to Elinor.

"I actually am going to see if Pam needs any help in the kitchen. She's been working her butt off," said Red Glasses. "So go say hi to them."

"Okay," said Elinor. "Well, it was nice talking to you!"

"Nice talking to you too! 'Hey girl, lol.' Hilarious!" said Red Glasses. "So funny, I have to tell Pam."

Peter started tugging Elinor toward J.W. and Sean, who were standing near the sideboard. Elinor watched Red Glasses and Bruce drift into the kitchen. Was it awkward for Mike's mother to know she was Internet dating? Maybe it made her look cool, she couldn't tell. In any case, it was typical Peter to stop the whole thing short before either result had been established.

Sean and J.W. were talking to a man with a beard (was it Richard Cooley? It looked like him but Elinor couldn't know for certain), and purposefully keeping their backs to Elinor and Peter, so that they were not allowed entrance into the conversation. She heard J.W. tell the bearded man, "Well, she has a lot of baggage. That's undeniable." He looked more ebullient than she had ever seen him.

"What are you doing here?" Elinor hissed at Peter. She poured herself a glass of wine off the sideboard.

"What?" said Peter. He looked dazed. Elinor could see a fleck of ketchup on one of his sleeves.

"How were you invited to this?"

"Well, it's not like you are the only guest, you know."

"I know that!" said Elinor. "But why are you all here?"

"Well, on Friday, I asked Sean what he was doing this weekend and he told me about this party. I just said, 'I think I should go too,' and Sean said yes. What are you doing here? Aren't you and Mike broken up?"

"We are! But that doesn't mean I can't go to this."

"I was hoping to hang out with Mike," said Peter ruminatively. "Where is he?"

"He's not here yet," snapped Elinor. She reached down to a side table filled with hors d'oeuvres and took a bite out of a filo pastry. It had spinach and cheese inside and was still partially frozen.

"Well, I hope he shows up!" said Peter. "I was looking forward to hanging out with him. I haven't seen him in forever."

"I hate you," said Elinor.

"Why are you saying that?" said Peter. "That is really inappropriate to say to a mentor."

"*You* are inappropriate!" said Elinor. She was going to say more, but Mike had arrived. He was talking to his father and his arm was close to (but not touching) Andrea, who was wearing a long T-shirt as a dress.

There is perhaps nothing more dispiriting than things going extremely differently from how you rehearsed them in your mind. Of all Elinor's fantasies about this evening, none of them included Andrea showing up wearing a long T-shirt as a dress. But as she looked closer, Elinor realized that the woman she thought was Andrea wasn't Andrea at all. She was taller and prettier than Andrea, her eyebrows were larger, and she had a fanciful tattoo above her elbow. Was it a house? Was it a pentagram?

"Mike is here," said Peter.

"I know, I see him," said Elinor. She watched Mike's mother walk out of the kitchen (Red Glasses and Bruce were absent) and embrace Mike. She even shook the Andrea look-alike's hand.

"I'm going to say hi to him," said Peter.

"You are?"

"Do you want to come?"

"Yeah, I want to come!" said Elinor. "I was going to say hi anyway."

"Okay, well, I'm going now."

"Fine," said Elinor. Peter scaled the room rather quickly, and Elinor trailed behind him, feeling an increasing amount of anger at Andrea's identical twin. Why was she here? It was so inappropriate to just barge into a family party like this. She wished she could have texted Sheila about it. For the merest second, Elinor grieved the fact that they weren't speaking.

"Hey, Mike," said Peter. He had approached Mike's right side. Andrea's clone was talking to Mike's mother. Elinor was behind all of them. Mike didn't seem to register that she was there.

"Peter, it's been forever, how are you, man! It's good to see you." Mike slapped Peter on the back and embraced him around the shoulders. He still didn't seem to see Elinor.

"Hey, Mike," said Elinor, loudly.

"Oh hey," said Mike, but not in a surprised way. Maybe he had seen her before but was trying not to make a big thing out of it.

"I read your piece on Iran," said Peter.

"Yeah, well." Mike ran his hands through his hair. "Sure,

the agreement has problems in a lot of ways, but what are the alternatives?"

Elinor looked at Fake Andrea, talking to Mike's mother. Fake Andrea had a cartilage earring. Elinor had had a cartilage earring in eighth grade too, but it just kept closing up.

"How's Journalism.ly?" Mike asked Peter.

"It's great," said Peter. "I've been doing a lot of writing. And I work with Elinor."

"Uh, yeah, I know," said Mike.

Elinor smiled at Mike. She felt a flush of gratefulness to him for remembering where she worked.

"Uh, how is it there?" said Mike. He cast a spasmodic glance at Andrea's doppelgänger, who was still chatting with his mother.

"It's amazing," said Peter. "J.W.'s starting to write an opinion column. It's called 'Thoughts and Musings.' And I'm pioneering our new gaming initiative."

"Cool," said Mike.

"And I'm doing a bunch of stuff too," said Elinor, louder again. "I've been writing personal essays."

Mike didn't look at her.

"Elinor has become really interested in feminism," said Peter. "I'm mentoring her. She was just on TV, so—"

Elinor felt a buzzing in her ears as if she were tumbling over a concrete ledge.

"I was just talking about online dating with one of your mom's friends," said Elinor, her vision narrowing, her breath becoming shallower. "And just about like, how many disrespectful messages women get when they are just trying to represent their bodies in the digital space. I might write an essay about that."

Mike looked at the floor. Elinor couldn't tell what he thought about that. His eyes were fixed on the geometry of the rug below them.

"Is it true that Memo Points Daily is going out of business?" asked Peter.

"What?" Mike's gaze shot up.

"I've heard rumors," said Peter, in his oxenish way.

"I think I would know," said Mike, sharply.

Mike's mother had wandered off toward the kitchen again, and Andrea Jr. stood on the other side of Mike, looking as if she wanted entrance into the conversation. Elinor couldn't tell if she was pleased this wasn't actually Andrea or sort of frightened by it. Were there that many people who were clones of Andrea? Did this mean that Mike was dating only people who looked like Andrea? Or was he just friends with them?

"Uh, this is Fiona."

"Hi, Fiona," said Elinor, immediately and inwardly congratulating herself on her civility.

"She works at Memo Points."

"Cool!" said Elinor. "Do you know Andrea?"

"It's a big company," said Fiona apologetically. She tugged at the arm of her T-shirt dress.

"Fiona, do you want to get a drink?" said Mike. He steered her away from the group.

. . .

Peter and Elinor stayed for fifteen minutes longer at the party, then they took an Uber back together. Peter said he needed to go in the direction of Astoria. Ordinarily, it would have pissed Elinor off that she had to share an Uber with a man she'd told she hated him a mere forty-five minutes before, but at this point, she was too anxious to care. Had going to the party been a good idea? Elinor couldn't tell. It was good to see Mike's mother. In truth, Elinor had thought the whole thing would have gone differently. Had anyone even read her viral essay? At least she thought Mike would have. Of course they didn't need to read her piece, but it did like, go viral. It was weird that no one said anything.

"Did you have a good time at the party?" asked Elinor, after the car door closed.

"I did, it was good to see Mike. He's a good guy. Although Memo Points Daily might literally shut down, it's doing so badly."

"Yeah," said Elinor, feeling, all of a sudden, like she was going to cry.

"I had a good ride to the party with Sean and J.W.," said Peter.

"That's cool," said Elinor, not really listening. She closed her eyes.

"Is something wrong?" said Peter.

"It was hard for me to see Mike tonight. I think?"

"You guys seemed like you were getting along well."

"Yeah," said Elinor. "I mean, maybe we were? So maybe going to the party was a good idea."

"I think so," said Peter. "I think we did some good networking."

They rode in silence. Elinor looked out the window until Peter got out at his subway stop.

. . .

Days later, alone in her apartment eating Chinese food, Elinor
got an email from Mike.

> Dear Elinor,
>
> Good seeing you at the party. I was wondering if you wanted
> to get a coffee sometime, maybe to catch up? I haven't seen
> you in a while and I would love to get an update on how you're
> doing.
>
> Mike

For months, Elinor had wondered what she would do if she
ever got an email of any kind from Mike. Now that it had
finally happened, she was numb, but triumphant. Her appearance at the party had worked. Talking about online dating with
Mike's mother's friends was not an impulsive and tragic mis-
step but, instead, the instinctive maneuver of a Duke of Wel-
lington. He had missed her!

It was at times like these she wished she could talk to Sheila,
for though their friendship had its downturns and trials, it
was ultimately a good source of sympathy. No one else had
the ability to say nothing anxiety provoking at all over such
an extended length of time. Sheila had a particular gift in that
way.

Elinor decided to look at Sheila's Instagram. She hadn't
looked at it in the past couple of weeks, out of anger.

Sheila had posted a new picture recently. It was a selfie of
Sheila in her scrubs. And it had this caption:

Its weird to be sleeping in the hospital as a visitor when you
usually work all night in one #imusedtoallnighters #GoRalph

The location on the picture said she was at NYU Hospital.

Did something bad happen to Ralph? Elinor clicked on the
hashtag #GoRalph, but all that came up was pictures of someone's wedding in Indiana. She decided to comment on Sheila's
Instagram.

"Hey! What happened to Ralph? Are you okay?"

Elinor took a bite of Chinese food and heard her phone
buzz. Sheila had responded to her comment.

"He's at NYU Hospital for a while :(."

Elinor commented on Sheila's comment. "Omg!!! Is he ok?"

Elinor's phone buzzed again.

"He's fine, but sick. I'm visiting him now."

Elinor decided then and there that she would go to the hospital. Some people would probably not contact Sheila during
her time of need because of the petty differences between them,
but Elinor wasn't one of those people. She would go to Sheila
now and help her. Because sometimes people need to act. She
would even take an Uber.

In case you were wondering or keeping tabs, these two recent
Ubers were relative anomalies. Since she lived in Queens, Eli-
nor had been taking the subway way more. She had basically
broken her obsessive cab habit. She had a lot more money now.
It was how she had a new pair of boots from Zappos.com. The
Uber was simply a treat for her good deed.

Once she got to NYU's main building, she walked straight
up to the receptionist. The room had the peculiarly rank scent

of hospital food even though there didn't seem to be a cafeteria anywhere.

"Hey! I'm here to visit Ralph Eisen?"

"Visiting hours are over?" said the woman. "Sorry."

"But I know my friend is here, she just published an Instagram from his bedside, so. She's definitely here."

"I'm sorry. Visiting hours ended two hours ago."

"Okay," said Elinor.

She texted Sheila. "Hey! I'm at the hospital right now. Are you here?"

Elinor saw a cloudy bubble with dots in it appear on her phone. She looked at her last text. It was a month ago. She would have been heartless, she thought, if she didn't feel a stab of compunction at that.

Sheila finally wrote back! "Hey, you're here? Me too! Are they being bitches about visiting hours? I'll come down and get you."

"Thanks!" texted Elinor. She included the final exclamation point on purpose to seem friendly.

Sheila came down the stairs about ten minutes later. She was still in her scrubs. They were pink. She had her hair pulled back into a ponytail. Elinor ran toward her and hugged her.

"Oh my god," said Elinor. "I came as soon as I saw your Instagram. What the fuck happened?"

"Oh my god," said Sheila. She walked over to the plastic leather chairs that populated the waiting room and sat down in one. Elinor followed. "This is so nice of you to come. Thank you. I mean, this has just been my nightmare for the last week. And like, two days ago Ralph's parents were in town and I finally met them. It's just been so insane. And on top of that

I've been working. I mean, luckily he's here, so I can look in on him, but still. It's just been ridiculous."

"So, honestly, what happened? All of a sudden Ralph's in the hospital? I literally couldn't believe it. That's why I rushed here—"

"Yeah, it was insane. Ralph actually got hit by a bus?"

"What? What?" said Elinor. "Oh my god, I can't believe that. What?"

"I know, it's unreal. He was just crossing the street and then he literally got hit by a bus. I mean, it's *crazy.* He's in traction. He broke both of his femurs."

"Oh no!"

"I mean, nothing happened to his head, thank god. But he is suing the city."

"Wow," said Elinor. "How did he survive?"

"Well, the bus wasn't going that fast. And he was on a Citi Bike. I told him he could sue Citi Bike too."

"That's good." Elinor imagined Ralph's body bouncing off a bus like a balloon off a wall. "Listen, I'm so sorry about our fight."

"I'm sorry too," said Sheila. They hugged over the metal armrest separating the two chairs. "I'm so sorry we fought."

"I've just been stressed lately, I know that's not an excuse."

"I mean, me too," said Sheila. "It's been so stressful."

"But like, I just want you to know that we are actually best friends, okay? And you are really important to me!"

"You are really important to me too," said Sheila. Her eyes filled with tears. Then Elinor's eyes also filled with tears. Who else could she really talk to? It was Sheila or nothing.

"But the minute I realized you were here, I immediately just came here."

"I know," said Sheila. She wiped her eyes. "That was so sweet of you. That's why you are such a good friend."

"How long is he going to need to recover?"

"Probably like, twenty weeks. Do you want to see him?"

"Can I? The receptionist was like, no!"

"I'll just bring you up, whatever," said Sheila. "I'm actually off my shift now, I was just chilling here visiting. Rowena?" she called to the receptionist. "Can she come up with me?" The receptionist nodded.

Elinor followed Sheila down a green hallway and into an elevator that went up two floors. Once they got out of the elevator, they walked down another green hall, to a small room. Ralph was lying on an adjustable bed. His feet were held up over his head by small pulleys.

"Hey, Ralph?" said Sheila. "Elinor came to see you."

"Hi, El," said Ralph. He sort of smiled.

"He's on a lot of pain meds," said Sheila. "They are letting him out of the hospital in like, a week."

"Where's he going to go?" said Elinor.

"Well, see, I don't want you to get mad at me or anything?"

"I won't!" Elinor looked at Ralph. His eyes were half closed. His chin was as swollen as an overfed child's.

"But we've just been spending a ton of time together in the hospital, and you know how I was like, 'Let's move in, but just as friends,' before the accident but it didn't work out for some reason."

"Yes," said Elinor.

"Well, so we were talking when he came to the hospital and like, immediately he called me, and I rushed right over and we were talking and he was just like, 'Listen, I want to be with you.' Like, he actually said that. I wouldn't have done this if he didn't say it. So we decided that he would stay at my place, and recover. And I know you said that you didn't think he should move in, but I just felt like—"

"No, no, Sheila. Listen, I get it! I think that makes total sense."

Ralph started to snore, very loudly.

"Should we get out of here and let him sleep?" said Elinor.

"No, no," said Sheila. "He's fine. He's a super sound sleeper because of all the drugs he's on. So it's not even a big deal. So, yeah, that's what we're doing and I'm really happy about it."

"I'm really happy for you too!" said Elinor, and she really meant it. Of course there was a part of her that didn't want to say anything after the fight they'd just had—but she also didn't want to fight with Sheila because it did seem, in a bright, brittle way that almost certainly resembled madness, that Sheila was happy. And how was Elinor supposed to judge what made Sheila happy? Maybe that was actually more feminist, not to judge. There was certainly a satisfaction in her own open-mindedness and changeling opinions.

"I mean, I can't even say anything," said Elinor. "Whatever happens will happen? I mean, Mike actually wants to meet up."

"What?" said Sheila. "OMG OMG OMG! *What?*"

"I don't know," said Elinor. "Should I meet him?"

"OMG!" said Sheila. "Do you feel like you want to?"

"I do!" said Elinor.

"Then I think you should meet him!"

Elinor and Sheila talked about their respective reunions for about an hour. Sheila was a very attentive and sympathetic listener. It felt good to talk, finally. Sheila didn't judge her, and

she didn't judge Sheila. That was the best part about their
friendship.

. . .

Elinor texted Mike as the subway was inching overground,
right near a building that had a sign striding across the top of it
advertising a law office. The air outside was gray.

> Hey Mike! Thanks so much for the kind words. Yes, I would love
> to get a drink sometime. Name the day.

Maybe "Name the day" was a little much? But whatever, she
had already sent it. It was probably fine.

Mike wrote back right away.

> Hey E! Great to hear from you. Are you free on Tuesday? I'm
> going to be in Queens anyway because I'm going to a drinks
> thing in Long Island City. That's where you live, right? I can
> meet you in Long Island City if you want.

Long Island City? She actually lived really far away from
there, but still, why was he suggesting Queens? Best not to
think about things you can't control, thought Elinor, who
promptly thought about it constantly.

. . .

On Tuesday, Elinor wore her best underwear to work, a black
lace pair that didn't have any holes. She didn't think that she
and Mike were going to hook up or anything, but you should

wear underwear to empower yourself, which was what she was doing.

The workday was slow, and punctuated by Elinor moving around in her seat all the time because her underwear was very uncomfortable. Midway through the day, Elinor realized that she had them on inside out. While in the bathroom to change them, she looked at her outfit in the rimless, speckled mirror someone had recently hung off the bathroom door. She looked cool, she thought. A shapeless top she had seen on Instagram, jeans, boots, a drawstring bag. She really was a totally different person now—a journalist. Maybe that was something that Mike had realized while at the party.

Elinor got to Long Island City forty-five minutes before she was technically supposed to arrive. It was an unseasonably cold day, but Elinor was still dressed too warmly. She sweat a little into her sweater.

Elinor eventually found a coffee shop near where she was supposed to meet Mike. She sat on a cold metal chair and sipped on an almond milk latte. Occasionally, and with a sort of plodding obsessiveness that even she found embarrassing, she would check and recheck Mike's social media presence. His Snapchat story today was Tomas eating a sandwich. His Instagram this week was a funny misspelled sign. It was all adding up to a theory Elinor was developing and getting increasingly excited about. Andrea was not appearing on any of Mike's social media channels half as much anymore. Plus she didn't go to Mike's mother's party. Her demonic clone did. Were Andrea and Mike not hanging out as much?

Despite walking exceedingly slowly and stopping to read a

historical plaque, Elinor still arrived too early at the bar. But the bar was not a bad place to wait—it had wooden booths and pink walls. The cocktails had egg whites in them and grenadine. Elinor sat down at the counter, put her large drawstring bag on the floor next to her barstool, and ordered a drink.

"Can I have the Old Man at the Side of the Road?" she said to a bartender. The bartender was wearing a flannel shirt and had an evenly trimmed beard. Elinor tried to inject some coquettishness into her tone. "Or what do you like."

"The Old Man at the Side of the Road is a good drink," said the bartender. Then he busied himself with assembling the elements of the drink. He whipped an egg in a tiny silver eggcup. He added several dark-colored poultices. He even took a lime and swiped it along the rim of her tiny coupe cocktail glass for no discernible purpose. Why did Mike want to meet her someplace this nice? They never went somewhere so nice when they were dating.

Eventually, the bartender gave her the cocktail, which now resembled a light pink sherbet. Elinor was just taking a picture of it when Mike came up behind her and patted her on the shoulder.

"Hey, E," he said.

"Oh my god! How are you?" Elinor put her phone down next to her cocktail.

"I'm good, I'm good," said Mike. "Do you want to get a table?"

"Uh, yeah, sure!" That was when Elinor realized that in her excitement she had tipped over her bag, and several quotidian objects—crumpled receipts, a small leather pouch that had absolutely nothing in it, an empty tampon applicator (but where was the tampon?)—had all fallen out of it. Luckily, Mike had already turned around and was being led to a table by a waitress. Elinor crouched next to the barstool, put the tampon applicator back into her bag, and ran to catch up with Mike and the waitress, who were congregating around a two-person table. Mike indicated via a waving of the hand that Elinor should actually take the booth side. Mike was going to sit on a wooden stool. She never remembered Mike doing this type of thing before.

"So how are you?" said Mike. Under the circular glass lights hanging from the ceiling, the hollows below his eyes looked darker. He was even wearing a green sweater over his usual T-shirt.

"I'm good," said Elinor. "I'm just working a lot. Mostly."

"Did you have a good time at the party?"

"I did!" said Elinor. "It was nice to see everyone again."

"I'm glad you had fun."

"Did you have fun?"

"It was okay. In general, I hate going to that shit."

"Well, I had fun," said Elinor. There was a silence.

"I was surprised you came."

"Why?" said Elinor. "I said I was going to come."

"I know you did. I know you said that." Mike drummed his fingers on the table. "But that was a while ago. I just didn't know you were going to come."

"My whole office went. Plus I said I was going to come."

"That's true," said Mike, doubtfully. "It was good to see Peter."

"Yeah," said Elinor. "He's fine. How's Memo Points Daily?"

"Well, uh, it's good, uh—"

"What?"

"It's closing. They just told us."

"Oh, Mike," said Elinor, resisting the impulse to cover his hand with her hand. "I'm so sorry."

"Yeah, I mean, I wasn't that surprised. Honestly, it's good. I didn't know if I wanted to stay there forever. We had to file all the time, which really doesn't allow me to pursue all the long projects I really want to pursue. And since now the party infrastructure has selected their nominees—"

"Yeah, I know."

"Although, honestly, they are both so bad, I don't know which one is better—"

"Oh, Mike—"

"So there's a lot of stuff I want to do related to the election that I couldn't have done if I had stayed there. It's fine."

"Okay," said Elinor.

"It was cool to meet J.W. and Sean though. They seem like really nice guys. J.W. was telling me about his column."

"When did you talk to them?"

"I don't know." Mike blinked. "After you left I guess."

"Oh, okay," said Elinor. She changed the subject. "Where are you living now?"

"Well, I was living with my mom for a while. Then I moved to kind of Williamsburg area. I know, I know, it's douchey. It's not actually Williamsburg, it's more like Greenpoint. They just called it Williamsburg in the ad. Probably to get more rent, which is funny because I would have paid more rent to not live in Williamsburg."

"Is the apartment nice?" said Elinor. That was a dull question, she realized. She scratched her head.

"Yeah, it's pretty nice. We have like, windows and a living room. The kitchen's been redone, so that's pretty cool. We have a dishwasher—"

"Do you have roommates?" said Elinor, interrupting him. She didn't want to hear tales of a dishwasher.

"Yeah," said Mike. "Just one though. Tomas!"

"Oh yeah, how is he?"

"He's good." Mike drummed his fingers on the table again. "You live in Queens? I figured it out when you posted that picture that was like #Queenslifestyle haha. That's why I picked this place."

"That was so nice of you!" said Elinor, gleefully picking up on this change of tune. The preceding part of the conversation had been making her feel very glum. But this was heartening news. He looked at her Instagram, just like she looked at his Instagram. It wasn't weird to look at each other's Instagrams. "Yeah, I live in Queens. I actually have a studio though. That's why I moved there. I want to move to Brooklyn."

The characterization of her apartment as a studio was not actually an untruth. In fact in the Craigslist ad, Kathy had termed it a "semi-studio," so if Peter ever said anything to Mike implying that her apartment wasn't a studio, she would just tell Mike—

"That's so great. A studio, wow!" said Mike.

"Yeah, I know. I love it. And the cool thing about it is that Astoria's really an up-and-coming neighborhood, so. Well, my apartment's basically in Astoria. It's kind of on the outskirts. But that's way cooler, actually."

"Yeah, completely." Mike looked past Elinor's head. Was he looking at the waitress? No, it was the window.

"It was good to see your mom the other night," said Elinor.

"She's freelancing for the *Times Magazine* now. She just wrote a big piece on Upper East Side adoptions."

"I read that!" said Elinor. She had tweeted her congratulations accordingly, and there had been a dearth of a reply.

"She read your essay too."

"Oh my god!" said Elinor. "Oh my god, that's so nice. She didn't even say anything at the party."

"Yeah, she told me she read it." Some ether of some feeling Elinor couldn't quite distinguish passed across Mike's face.

"Did you read it?"

"I read it."

"Well, what did you think about it?"

"Do you want me to be honest?"

"Um," said Elinor.

"Well, initially, I was kind of pissed. I was pissed you didn't ask me if you could write about me."

"I didn't mention you by name!" said Elinor, raising her voice, and feeling panic overwhelm her, as if she had fallen into a well. Mike shushed her.

"But then I thought—"

Elinor made a bleating sound and Mike shushed her again.

"You are allowed to write whatever you want, of course. I would hope that if you ever wrote about me again you would ask me, but I thought it was good that you wanted to explore why women are forced to write about their breakups."

"Really?" Elinor blushed. "Thank you!"

"But I guess, I just wanted you to know that, you know,

I'm not this typical broey male journalist who devalued your writing. I actually hate guys like that. That's my least favorite kind of guy."

"I don't think you are that kind of guy at all," said Elinor. "I never said that."

"I think I helped you," said Mike. "At least you gave me credit for that."

"Yeah," said Elinor. She was still very nervous. She felt an itch in the interior of her eye like it would never stop blinking. Her mind was a blank. All she could clearly determine was that she wanted him to stop talking about this. "I mean, nothing was messy. It was just a process where we grew and changed and felt like we were different people."

"But I just wanted to say, you know? You're a good writer."

"Thank you," said Elinor. "For saying I am a good writer. That means a lot."

"You're welcome," said Mike.

"Listen," said Elinor, grabbing Mike's hand. "I'm glad we could hang out. I've missed you. My years with you were so important. I really loved you." Elinor was worried her eyes were involuntarily filling with tears. This sometimes happened to her, and she hoped it wasn't happening to her now.

"Sure." Mike's phone buzzed audibly, rattling the table. He picked it up and looked at it, and Elinor saw the coldness he felt toward her so distinctly it jolted her like a slap. It surprised her, even after all of that.

"I'm sorry about that," said Mike. He put his phone down.

"No worries," Elinor said, too loud.

"So yeah, what were you saying?"

"Nothing that good."

. . .

They were outside the bar. Elinor had put on her coat inside the bar, but Mike was still putting his coat on, over his sweater.

"Wow," said Elinor.

"Yeah," said Mike. "It was really good to see you."

"It was supergood to see you too. Here! Come in for a hug!"

Mike approached Elinor and they hugged. She smelled Mike's coat. It smelled the exact same way that it used to, like pizza.

"Are you going to the reunion this summer?" said Elinor.

"Not sure. Especially with this job stuff," said Mike. He sighed. "Speaking of which, I hate to be a dick, do you know if there are any openings at Journalism.ly?"

"I don't know." The street they were on, Elinor realized, was deserted—an unusual thing in New York. She noticed that the bar didn't have many patrons, that paint was peeling off the wooden trim that encircled the roof. Maybe this bar was going to go out of business. It was a bad bar anyway. The Old Man at the Side of the Road was a terrible drink, despite its pink color. "I don't think so."

"Not that I want to work there. I was just wondering," said Mike. "And also like, would I have to write about all this stuff I didn't want to write about?"

"We have a politics section." Elinor thought of the Journalism.ly's antiseptic politics section. She still had never spoken to Josh, whose bald spot had grown precipitously. Then she thought about Mike, working alongside Josh, wandering into the kitchen, pouring himself a cup of coffee, and wandering out of it.

"The thing is, though," said Elinor quickly. "I'm not sure you could really do it."

"What?"

"Well, it's way different than what you're doing now."

"How so?"

"You have to reach a big audience, Mike, you know? I don't know you can really do that."

"You mean like, I kind of write very rarefied stuff?"

"No!" said Elinor. "You don't have a social media following, and that's a big part of the job. Like, you never even put anything up."

"Okay." Mike scratched his arm. "But I don't think that's that hard to do. I could put stuff up if I wanted to."

"Also like, I share a lot of stuff in my writing. I'm very honest—and I feel like Journalism.ly is really about realness."

"And you think I'm not real?" Mike was surprised, she could tell.

"No. That's not what I'm saying. I'm saying I don't think you would like working there because I just don't think you would like it."

"Okay."

"Plus we don't have spots anyway."

"Oh, okay, whatever . . ." Mike's voice trailed off.

"Sorry! I'm just trying to give you a heads-up."

"Yeah, thanks for telling me. That doesn't sound like something I'd be interested in," said Mike.

"I'll email you if I hear anything though! Bye!"

"See you around," said Mike. "Bye!"

Interestingly enough, they never saw each other again. Mike

never followed up on the job and Elinor never emailed him. It was the end.

. . .

On the subway ride back home, Elinor's mind pored over the preceding events. In the end, she didn't know how to think about it. She felt slightly depressed, but perhaps that was irrational.

When the train finally went overground, she texted Sheila. "Meeting Mike was great! He totally apologized to me for how he acted and I really feel like we're friends now. Meeting up was just a good thing to do."

"OMG," Sheila texted, two hours later.

ACKNOWLEDGMENTS

There are so many people who have contributed to this book, and I am incredibly blessed to work with a tremendous team.

I have to specifically thank my editor, Jenny Jackson, whose absolutely brilliant edits transformed this book into what it is. She read so many drafts (literally so many, I have lost count) and always had something trenchant, incisive, and revolutionary to say. She helped me zero in on the core of Elinor and relentlessly pushed me for the more subtle insight, the larger point, the deeper meaning. She gave shape to the book and never lost faith. Her unfailing support was what got me through the process.

I love Doubleday! Thank you so much, Zakiya Harris, for always clarifying what I meant when I did a terrible and incoherent cross-out. Thanks also to Lauren Weber, who has been extremely helpful in bringing me into the twenty-first century.

To my agent, Jane Finigan—you are the best. Thank you for molding this book with your extreme intelligence as you always do. You are such a sharp reader and a great friend. I feel privileged that you read my books!

To David Forrer, thank you so much for being so helpful in

a million ways. You rock. I'm so immensely grateful to you and the entire team at Inkwell.

To everyone at Lutyens and Rubinstein, especially Felicity, Sarah, and Juliet. Thank you so much. I have loved talking with you all about the issues this book tackles and I am so happy to have such brilliant, funny, and amazing representation.

To my family and husband. I love you guys! I bet you are all glad to stop talking about social media's implications for post-modernism, and I am too. It's depressing!